Gravity Comics Massacre

Vincenzo Bilof

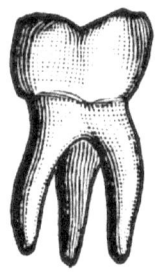

Bizarro Pulp Press
www.BIZARROPULPPRESS.com
Gravity Comics Massacre Copyright © 2013 Vincenzo Bilof
Cover art by Justin T. Coons

ISBN-10: 0615843387
ISBN-13: 978-0615843384

Other stuff Vincenzo Bilof wrote

Necropolis Now
Queen of the Dead
Nightmare of the Dead
The Horror Show
Confessions of the Impaler
Mother, I'm Not an Android (I Promise)
Japanese Werewolf Apocalypse

GRAVITY COMICS MASSACRE

a.k.a. Fuck Everything and Read a Comic Book Because the Aliens Look Cool When They're Drawn by a Professional Artist

PROLOGUE AND EPILOGUE

Skinning was hard work, especially when the victim was still alive, although that didn't make it any less fun. Damien regretted he hadn't been able to find a woman for a long time. He preferred the tall, slender middle-class women who felt their futures were secure. They were fun to chop into pieces because even until their last breath, they still believed someone was going to save them.

He didn't particularly care for torture, but today, he was in the mood for it. The little Indian boy who'd been left for drunk on the side of the road by his buddies was in for one hell of a time, but at the very least, Damien would get what he wanted. The kid would experience one of his wildest dreams—in the flesh, of course.

Currently, the teenager sniveled and sobbed under duct tape, choking with his red, runny eyes focused intently on the fat man. Damien had no illusions about his weight issue—his mother told him once long ago that people would always find a way to judge him because of his size. So, it was best to embrace his physical 'deformity.' The truth of the matter was that most people didn't understand how lucky he really was to have so much flesh.

Damien never cared much for clothes, even when his comic store was still open. Folds of fat jiggled over his soiled underwear, while a forest of hair on his thighs and chest curled in a swampy disaster of sweat and dirt. Damien stomped around the dusty, old store with a pen in his hand, habitually running his fingers along his hair.

"This is always so exciting," he stopped in front of the man and squeezed his hands together. "You see, Mr. Grayson—I'm going to call you that—um, well, this is an opportunity for you. When I started doing this, I had a lot of help. I wasn't quite sure what I wanted, so it was a bit messy. Now I know *exactly* what I want, and that makes this a whole lot easier for both of us. I usually only chop up women, but for everyone else, they get something a lot more special."

Mr. Grayson screamed against the duct tape.

Damien burst with a sudden laugh. "What the hell is your problem? It's not really that big of a deal! You see this pen in my hand? There's a story behind this pen. Now, you're sitting in the finest comic book store in the state of Arizona. It's the one attraction this shitty town has."

Damien gestured at the empty, cobwebbed shelves of *Gravity Comics,* and the windows caked with grime and some yellow, un-nameable substance that had been smeared across the glass. Meager light penetrated that wall of detritus and rot—just enough to reveal the cowering Indian boy who'd been unlucky enough to have wandered off his reservation with a bunch of friends and left on the side of the road as a joke.

"They had their eyes on me for a long time." Damien began to recount the tale, as he always liked to do. He had a flair for the dramatic; it was very likely he

6

was previously incarnated as Edgar Rice Burroughs, or in the very least, Marlon Brando. He was a storyteller and an artist, but for most of his life, he'd been misunderstood.

"My mother knew them very well, you see. These friends of ours used to come and visit regularly, and they eventually explained they were the ones who inspired Stan Lee, and Phillip K. Dick. You know who I'm talking about, right?"

Grayson, of course, found it difficult to respond.

Damien sighed. "Fucking, Christ. I hate ignorance. I really do. And you know what? I'm not a big fan of torture, because it's *so* boring. It's overdone! You're expecting torture, aren't you? You're sitting there, pissing yourself, and you think I'm a sick fuck who's going to torture you. Well, guess what, Dick Grayson! Torture's fucking BO-RING. But you… YOU! I'm thinking about it. I really am. Only, I'm not all that good. I don't know anatomy or anything, so I might kill you before I'm actually done. That would piss me off."

Damien paced back and forth in an attempt to restart his story. "I was talking about the aliens. They were also the ones who helped write a bunch of religious stuff, too, but we're not here to talk about that garbage! I mean, I don't get it! How can you believe in God and not believe in aliens?" Damien had been pacing back and forth. He sharply turned to face Mr. Grayson, and roared, "Did you hear WHAT I SAID? HOW CAN YOU BELIEVE IN GOD AND NOT ALIENS? Have you been listening? Aliens are behind everything! They're the ones who created all

7

our favorite superheroes! So they were responsible for the success of my store, in a way. It was their idea in the first place. I grew up with these aliens, and they have a name, but that's too complicated for you. I can see I'm already over your head."

Damien pulled up a chair opposite his prey, scraping it against the floorboards that had been stripped of bloodstained carpet long ago. He drooled into the forest of curly, black hair on his chest while retrieving his clipboard from the counter. He sat his bulbous body down into the chair.

"I'll do the work," he grumbled to himself. "They want their data, after all. Don't worry about me, I can see just fine. I promise we won't be interrupted. My friends have done all they can to separate us from the rest of the world. Nobody will come for you because they can't see us! Not detectable by satellites, visible only to the naked eye. Speaking of eyes…" Damien's tone became introspective and professorial, like a professor of literature poring over a graphic novel while attempting to discern its educational value. "I wonder what goes on when you close yours? What're your nightmares like, Mr. Grayson? Tell me about them, but don't do it with your lips. Allow me to watch you squirm as your worst fear comes true. It's not for me to know, but you see, my liege lords require data to help them continue with their analysis of the human psyche. They require your fear, and in exchange, I get to decorate my wondrous store."

With the pen that his benefactors gave him, he began to sketch out a rough draft of the unfortunate young man. Damien didn't know exactly how the pen worked, only that the device could make a man realize his fears. Whatever horrible sensations Mr. Grayson envisioned awaited him; the data was crucial to the success of the benign experiment. It didn't matter what the experiment was; Damien was fulfilling his destiny.

Damien was an excellent artist; he should have been drawing comics for DC ages ago, but they didn't realize how talented he was.

He sucked drool into his mouth while studying the writhing victim. When the drawing was finally finished, he retrieved his toolbox and brought it into the room. It was time to wallpaper the room.

The Indian boy dreamed.

***

Cheveyo sat on the worn couch in the trailer where he lived with his mother, three sisters, and grandmother. Any minute now, his boys would be coming to pick him up for a night at the bar. Rosie the bartender was working tonight. He pretended to be confident in front of his friends that she would eventually capitulate to his advances. He wrote her poems and bought her flowers, but she kept up her snide remarks—poured his shots with a smirk on her face while she listened to him rant about how beautiful she was. At least she was always nice enough to call a cab whenever his friends ditched him.

Out of the corner of his eye, a flash of movement skittered across the threadbare carpet. A trick of perception, nothing more. He continued to play with his smart phone, checking for a text message from one of his buddies because they were running late. More movement to his peripheral prompted him to turn again and scan the floor. No one was in the trailer but him. The room's silence allowed him to feel the speed of his heartbeat. He returned his gaze to the barren land outside the window, and only a moment later, he glimpsed a shape race across the floor and disappear beneath the sofa.

Cheveyo felt ridiculous. Tiny creatures or objects that moved quickly reminded him of spiders, and his sensitivity to arachnophobia often had him look away from shadowy corners. Spiders could easily hide in dirty, dusty environments that were rarely touched by human hands. Looking beneath the sofa was hardly an attractive proposition, but it was the only way to stop his heart's incessant hammering. Rosie knew he had a fond distaste for spiders and often made jokes about his weakness.

It was time to 'man-up' and get his shit together. Rosie would want a strong man, not a little piss-ant who was afraid of creepy crawlies.

He took a deep breath and leaned over the edge of the couch to peer underneath.

At first, they looked like furry hands. Cheveyo stopped breathing. Reality seemed to have paused. His brain processed the black stripes across the long, spindly legs. He blinked. He blinked again. And again. A million eyes stared back at him from the fissure between the couch and the floor. He wanted to move, but his body wouldn't respond. He couldn't hear anything but Rosie's voice in his head, calling him a pussy.

He curled up into a ball on the corner of the couch. His hands closed into tight balls that he couldn't open, his fingertips cold, his lips unmoving. He couldn't tear his eyes away from the edge of the cushions; he waited. He tested his sanity and waited while his eyelids refused to fall. It would have been better to look away, to tell himself that it wasn't real, but his entire body was held in stasis, and all sensation was terminated. He couldn't feel the cold fingertips anymore, and his heartbeat faded as blood rushed to his head and filled his ears.

The first flesh-colored arachnid trickled over the sagging middle cushion. It moved slowly and deliberately. It spanned the width of a man's hand. Stopping in the middle of the couch, it might have been staring at him, fearlessly judging him as a meek creature. The spider climbed over the top, and Chevyo wanted to follow it with his eyes; his fragmented consciousness demanded a course of action. He should retrieve a weapon, or run, or wake the FUCK UP. But it was no use.

His lips parted only slightly to allow a shallow exhalation that should have been a scream.

Another spider, a twin to the first, rambled over the floor toward the sofa. Two more followed after it. Several more emerged from beneath the sofa and blanketed its surface, creating a forest of fuzzy legs. They were silent and watchful, methodically creeping over the upholstery.

Cheveyo didn't feel the piss that filled the

11

crotch of his jeans. His neck unfroze, and he turned only slightly to see his cell phone vibrate against the floor. His friends were calling—everything was normal, after all. He sighed and closed his eyes. The spiders weren't real. Maybe he was an alcoholic, and he was starting to hallucinate as the result of shitty withdrawal symptoms. At the very least, this was just a bad dream... a bad dream...

He opened his eyes again when he felt something jerking on his pant leg, imploring him to pay attention. He watched as hundreds of hand-sized, tiger-striped spiders crawled over the ceiling and along the walls. His bowels loosened completely, and his pants filled up.

One of them climbed over his leg and perched atop his knee cap.

Cheveyo finally screamed, though no one could hear him.

THE FIRST CHAPTER

Her long legs were perched over the dashboard in the dull, brown world of desert dust. The colorless rendition of an American wasteland stretched neatly over miles of sun-stained horizon. Balls of dust pushed by the wind rolled across the scorched land where only lizards and loners in search of peyote Nirvana dared to appear within the power of the white sun, which hovered in its kingdom of sky and cloud. A sheen of sticky sweat clung to her smooth, tapioca legs. Strands of jet-black hair stuck to her forehead, while her parted lips and perpetually bored gaze stared at the nothing around them.

She had to know that Brian couldn't help but glance at her every few minutes. He pretended to be checking the passenger-side mirror, but of course, there was nothing but the hard plain behind and beyond them. She had to feel his eyes on her crossed ankles; he watched her tap her toes to a beat only she could hear. Miko, the Asian stripper who probably had a tragically shitty back story of her own, would never give him the time of day. She hadn't said one word to Brian since he picked everyone up for their fun little trip.

Marijuana smoke lingered on the thick, humid air in the van, staining the upholstery with its skunk-smell. Brian hated the smell of pot; he hated most smells, in fact. The heat made everything worse, and Kirk's beat-up white van with the seats in the back

13

removed didn't have functional air conditioning, which added to Brian's discomfort. He took his glasses off several times to wipe sweat out of his eyes.

The whole thing was a bad idea, and he regretted ever mentioning the abandoned town to Jack, whose head was always filled with wild ideas.

Jim Morrison's voice crooned over the radio.

"Light my fire!" Jack shouted from the back. "Turn this shit up, Brain!"

Brian Powers hated his nickname; it had followed him through school, and all the geniuses at the Ford dealership thought themselves profound intellectuals when they decided to call him Brain, because after all, he has 'BRAIN POWERS!'

But it was Jack who first coined the nickname on the playground during recess. Black-haired, swarthy Jack Murphy had a soft-spot for the kids who were bullied; he loved underdogs, a trend that always found him as the benevolent protector of the weak through all the different public schools his parents moved him between while he was busted for selling drugs, condoms, and alcohol.

Jack had pummeled two bigger kids whose names Brian couldn't remember, because for the rest of his life, there had been only Jack. The protector had become his world.

With his fists clenched, Jack had frowned for a moment while standing over the smaller boy. "Your name's… Brian?" he asked.

"Uh-huh," the boy wiped his mouth with the back of his hand while peering up at the powerful youth

14

who held the future in his hands.

"No." Jack laughed. "Your name's Brain. Brain Powers!"

Jack helped him to his feet, and ever since, Jack never had to do his own homework again.

Henceforth, the auto financial consultant will be referred to as Brain, because he is, indeed, smarter than the average human. At thirty, he possessed a full head of blond hair and was still exceptionally slim despite his lack of exercise. Brain was the underachieving sorcerer of numbers who preferred Anime porn—Hentai—to the company of real, flesh-and-blood women. He was effectively the loser who wanted to remain within the shadows of Jack's smoldering propensity to defy moral conventions. He was the four-eyed pencil-pusher and action-figure collector who watched science fiction shows that were almost always cancelled after one season. Whatever Jack wanted, Brain provided.

Including this silly trip, though he was the one who opened his mouth about the abandoned town.

The girl in the back of the van, Jamie, giggled while handing a Coke bottle mixed with the rum of their favorite pirate captain to Kirk, the bouncer who always rambled about his musical tastes and dreams of making it big with his own band, despite how awful of a musician he really was.

Kirk downed the bottle.

"Hey! Don't hog it all!" Jamie playfully punched her boyfriend in the shoulder. She was the blond drunkard who was likely going to take off her tank top to let her tiny breasts breathe. Even though she

15

wasn't a stripper like Miko, she hated wearing clothes, as evidenced by her lack of a bra and the perky little nipples that poked through the fabric of her thin top. Brain hated such trash. Miko was something else.

Don't look at her. Keep your eyes on the road.

"I don't even wanna go on this stupid trip!" Jamie pouted. "When we get back, I want you to buy my puppy. You promised me last week. You also promised for my birthday, and I'm *still* waiting."

"What's your problem?" Kirk shot Jamie a hard glare. "You wanna tell me what to do? Huh?"

It was a serious moment. They all knew that Kirk beat her as a matter of habit, and Brain alone knew that her and Jack were screwing whenever it was convenient. Whatever delusions she had with Jack, she should've known one thing about him: love wasn't his style.

The tension finally eased when Jack asked, "So are we gonna eat these pills, or put 'em up our noses? I've been waiting around for you two to stop your bullshit…"

"Noses," Kirk said with finality. "Oxy, right? Fuckin' HELL YEAH! How 'bout you Miko? Brain? You two down?"

Miko didn't say anything, and Brain shook his head. "Gotta drive."

"Whatever, man," Kirk said. "More for me. Hey, how come you ain't using GPS? How do you know where we're going?"

Brain sighed. "Look, let me drive. I can't concentrate with you guys shouting every three

16

seconds."

"Quit being such a bitch," Jack said.

"I just want to party," Kirk added. "It don't matter to me none."

Brain was worried Miko would think the whole trip was stupid. Why was she there in the first place? How much did Jack pay her? Jack was right though: he would need to loosen up a bit, at least try to act like a hardass. He knew the game, and damn it, he was an adult. He was a *man,* and he hoped Miko would see how much of a loser Jack really was and go with him instead. Brain was smarter and made his money the honest way. Jack paid for the stripper to amuse himself because he was their king; it was his demonstration of power.

"Aliens," Brain said. "Aliens scrambled the satellites around Hooksville. We can use an old-fashioned map, but that's it."

Everyone in the back seat erupted with laugher, but Miko kept her eyes focused on the road, clucking her tongue against the roof of her mouth. *Cluck. Cluck.*

"I *love* aliens, man," Kirk announced. "Take a hit of this, brother."

Jamie's shrill, girlish laughter overpowered Jim Morrison's voice on the radio as Kirk introduced a fifth of Jack Daniels, his hand clutched around the neck. This was the test. He wasn't doing drugs, but he would have to prove he was tough, or they would continue to shit all over him during the rest of the trip, and Miko would avoid him like the plague.

Automatically, he wanted to point out it was illegal to drive intoxicated, but at this point, it wasn't worth it. The van reeked and there were narcotics all over the damn place.

Brain grabbed the bottle and poured a long gulp of fiery liquor down his throat. *Don't throw up… don't throw up… don't throw up…*

He swallowed it and refused to grimace. As much as he hated alcohol, he knew what was at stake.

They hooted and hollered as Brain decided to grow a pair and offer the bottle to Miko, his first attempt at becoming visible in her world. Without looking at him, she grabbed the bottle and took an even longer swig. More hollering in the backseat was proof of their approval.

Why did Kirk and Jamie have to come at all? They were part of Jack's network of drug pushers, but they didn't need to come on the trip. Why was Miko here? Brain had never met her before, and he could scarcely peel his eyes away. She was a distraction, and he hated it. He wanted to go home and watch Hentai videos over and over again until he could sleep without dreaming.

Ahead of him and all around, there was the desert.

In the rearview mirror, Jack's deep, brown eyes glared. Brain wanted to go back in time, retract his story, and tell it to someone else or nobody at all. Who else existed for him but Jack, in all his glory and wisdom? Who else defended him against the injustices of the world? Who else was validated and in turn needed validation for every breath, for every step through the sleepy little shithole town where they lived—who else

18

needed Brain? Jack. Jack. Jack.

And so one day he told Jack the story about a mass-murderer…

***

"Fucking serial killers, huh?" Jack shrugged while shoving steak fries into his mouth. "That's what you're into these days?"

"Not a serial killer," Brain corrected him. "There's a difference. See, serial killers kill a lot of people in a series…"

"I get it, I get it." Jack looked around the empty pool hall, which also doubled as their town's most glamorous bar. It was usually empty at this time of day—lunchtime—but Jack was bored, which meant he was enduring the in-between state of a drug that made him anxious and another drug that slowed him down. Brain was more than familiar with Jack's sudden angst, and Brain was unofficially a safe zone.

Jack pushed the plate away after only eating a handful of fries, while Brain picked at a salad and scratched little doodles onto a napkin with his pen. The only person working in the place was Judy Trent, who had gone to school with them, and now had three kids. She worked long shifts serving drunks their food and their poison. Judy wiped down the bar and eyed the high school friends until Jack waved her over, never saying a word.

"You want a table?" Judy asked, her eyes flickering to the food he was surely going to waste. It was no secret she hated serving Jack; he was wasteful with food and rude to women. He regarded them as nothing more than a resource he could use at his disposal.

"What do *you* think?" Jack sat up impatiently and walked around the bar toward the pool cues that were lined up against the wall. Brain understood what was being asked of him. He glanced at his watch, thankful he had an hour lunch break.

Brain continued to snack on his salad while Jack broke the rack. While balls clattered around the table, some of them dropping into pockets, Brain couldn't help but wonder what the hell Jack wanted. He could tell his old friend was on edge; he had likely pumped far too many drugs into his body and didn't know what to do. He'd called Brain on a whim to ask out for lunch; they hadn't really spoken in a month, but that was Jack's way.

The TVs above the bar provided the only other sound while Jack ran the table. The Phoenix Coyotes were up for sale again, or they were going to move, or they were going to dissolve the team. Nobody ever seemed to know what was going on with an ice hockey team in the middle of the desert.

"You were saying?" Jack asked.

"What?" Brain said.

"Killers. That's what you've been up to. Reading. It's your shot, by the way. I scratched."

Brain took his shot and promptly knocked a ball into a side pocket while Jack chalked his stick like a madman. He stared at the TVs with false interest while

20

Brain missed his second shot.

"Um, yeah," Brain said. "You know, there're a lot of crazy things in Arizona nobody even knows about."

"You want to talk about aliens again?" Jack began to finish off the game.

"I can't believe you remember that."

"You were on an alien kick for about a year. Look, I'm itching to get out of this place. There's nothing to do around here. We need to open up other avenues... go somewhere else."

It was a conversation they had many times before. Everybody in town knew Jack, and he had a certain comfort level with both his rep and all the perks he earned from local businesses. He was hardly a gangster or a thug, but he was a man people respected.

"Talk about your aliens," Jack insisted. "Go on! Where are they? You want to go check out a crash site? Fuck man, I am *bored* out of my mind. I almost thought about getting married!"

"Married? You?"

"Yeah," Jack nodded. "There ain't shit to do around here. Let's go find some aliens and get absolutely wrecked on the way over, that way we really see aliens."

Brain was never interested in drugs, and he knew better than to get his hopes about up Jack's impulses. "I'm kind of over the whole alien thing," Brain said. "The government pretty much has that whole thing hushed up. Anyway, I learned about this crazy killer who shut down an entire town. Not a lot of people know about it. It happened right here in Arizona, and it

21

didn't get a lot of press for some reason."

"Rack 'em," Jack said after finishing off the eight-ball. "Keep talking."

"Sure. Well, about six years ago this guy had a comic book store, and he just suddenly went nuts one day. He closed up his store with some customers inside and chopped them up. He skinned them and stretched their skin over the windows and the walls. He had all the time in the world to do this, somehow. It's fucking crazy. The guy was never found, either. So the town kind of fell apart because everyone was afraid. Get this: three people went missing over the course of a month and their skin was found up in the comic store. I mean, nobody wanted to even burn the place down; everyone was scared out of their minds, so they all left. The town's abandoned. People think it's cursed."

Jack broke the rack again. "So, why don't we go then?"

"Go? To the town?"

"Sure. What else do we have to do? How far is it? We'll take a little trip."

"They never found the guy…"

"What's your point?" Jack's temper flared up. "You wanna go or not? When's the last time you took a vacation? I'll bring a girl, and we'll get you laid. I'll take care of you. I've got a couple ideas I want to go over. I'll need you to crunch all the numbers for me."

Now, Brain understood his friend's angle. "We can do that here. We don't have to go anywhere. You don't have to indulge me."

"I'm not indulging anybody," Jack bit his

22

bottom lip and leaned over the table to take his shot. "I need a distraction, and so do you. Sitting in your office all day reading about fucking killers…"

"They never caught him!" Brain repeated.

Jack played the role of genuine friend. "Who is this guy? Should I be looking for him on the street? Is there a reward if I help turn him in?"

Brain couldn't help but get excited. "His name's Damien Shears. He owned that comic store for almost twenty years. He was a pretty normal guy…"

"By normal you mean he lived alone and jerked off to comic books?"

Brain swallowed. "Well, he uh, he did live at his mom's, but she was committed to a nuthouse. She thinks she was abducted by aliens, and to this day, she keeps talking about the crazy experiments they used to do on her. In fact, I have a picture of her on my phone. Her name is—"

"There ya go!" Jack laughed. "Can't stay away from the aliens, can you?"

It was hard not to smile at Jack's expression. He was coming out of his funk with his own trademark shit-eating grin. Brain felt a sliver of optimism, but then again, it was just like Jack to promise the world and come through with nothing. He always had big dreams, and he was convinced Brain could somehow unlock the secrets to success, the hidden millions that were somehow, someway, his birthright. The universe owed Jack everything.

But Brain really didn't want to check out an abandoned town where a mass-murderer's ghost lingered. He'd rather go to a hockey game; at least there he could sneak furtive glances at the three or four hot moms who would be in attendance. If Jack wanted an adventure, it was much easier to go out for an evening so he could be back beneath his bed sheets with a Manga book on his lap.

"I'll bring Kirk and Jamie," Jack said. "Maybe I'll bring a special someone for you. I'll make an investment into our future together... you'll get laid, and then we'll get rich. An abandoned town is the perfect place for us to unwind, and plan."

"Kirk and Jamie?" Brain was surprised. "They're still together? Weren't you and Jamie screwing around? That sounds like a bad situation." The truth was that they were losers and Brain hated being around them. If it weren't for Jack, they wouldn't even be acquainted.

"What's your point?" Jack shrugged. "What difference does it make? She'll talk about puppies all day, and he'll cry about his music. They're good at partying."

"The whole thing's ridiculous!" Brain said. "Not even the FBI could find him! I have to request the time off. I have to let my mom know where I'll be..."

There was no arguing with Jack once his mind was made up. There was so much more to the story, but he could give a shit less. This was about some money-making scheme that was doomed to fail, like a dot.com or a hockey team in Mexico. The worse part about it was that Brain didn't want to leave for a week, especially because the new season of *American Ninja Warrior* was about to start.

24

Jack had every intention of visiting Hooksville in the middle of the desert, where a killer by the name of Damien Shears might still be hiding.

During their conversation, Brain had been mindlessly drawing on his napkin, unaware he was doing it at all.

"Haven't seen you draw anything in a long time," Jack remarked.

***

"Dude, fucking ghost town."

Kirk's superpowers included the innate ability to state the obvious better than anybody else. Since Jack hated going to nightclubs and concerts, Kirk had a lot of underground connections, but he preferred painkillers he could chop up and snort as his compensation. He used to think he was going to be a guitar player, so when he pulled an acoustic out of the back of the van Jamie, stumbled out after him. Brain shook his head.

"What's your problem?" Jack asked.

Brain shrugged, though his eyes caught a glimpse of long-legged, slender Miko, whose black blouse was halfway unbuttoned. Moisture glistened on her upper chest; Brain watched her tongue rove the edge of her upper teeth as she looked at the shattered, boarded-up buildings. After a few shots of Captain Morgan, his head was warm and the merciless sun made him want to throw up and take a nap, though he wasn't sure in what order.

25

"That's what I thought." Jack put a hand on his friend's shoulder. "Hot as balls out here. But look at this place… thanks to your alien friends, nobody comes here. Perfect place for a meth lab."

"Is this where Damien Shears killed all those people?" Kirk asked.

Suddenly, Kirk didn't seem like a simpleton, despite his classic Keanu Reeves haircut.

"You know who he was?" Brain asked.

"Everybody fuckin' knows," Kirk said. "Dude's a legend. Had the best comic book store in Arizona. I came here when I was a kid and bought Batman comics."

"Overrated," Brain said about the character. "I never understood what made him so special." It was best to talk; if all the noise ceased, you could hear the dreadful silence which lingered like the smell of a baby's diarrheic diaper.

"What're you talkin' about?" Kirk squared his shoulders aggressively. "Batman had to fight the baddest villains, man."

"That doesn't mean he was a good superhero," Brain pointed out. "He's got virtually unlimited resources, and through all the years, nobody could just shoot him in the head… just stupid…"

"Nerds," Miko said.

"Nerds are cute!" Jamie giggled and grabbed Kirk's shirt collar.

"Enough of this shit," Jack said while popping a cigarette into his mouth with his phone in his hand. "Cell phones really don't work out here, so Brain's right about

26

the aliens. I'll walk around and get the lay of the land. This is where it's all gonna start. This place." Melodramatically, he inhaled a deep breath, and exhaled. "Yeah. Smell that? That's the smell of success. We're going to move a mountain of cocaine and store it here. And meth too." He slapped Brain on the back.

"Okay, uh, well, I'll just hang out here with the van," Brain said.

"Fuck *that*," Kirk spat in the dirt. "There's nobody here, man. Going to find a church, break some windows, get this party started! WHOOO!" his holler echoed across the empty sky.

Perky-nippled Jamie danced away with Kirk down the empty street that had been conquered by dust. Vandals had broken the windows of old buildings and left their signatures scrawled in graffiti glory upon brick and wood. Signs had been weathered by time and the elements; burnt-out hovels loomed, casting shadows near the twisted metal frames of a few cars that had been stripped.

Uninterested in spelunking into the ruins of a ghost town, Brain leapt into the back of the van and listened to the buzzing in his head. His eyelids weakened, and the van's ceiling spun. The weed-smell crept into his nostrils, and he thought about Jack and his plan to set up a drug empire in the middle of nowhere. Jack would never admit he was a junkie.

He thought it was a drunken hallucination when he saw Miko sitting next to him in the van, rolling up another joint. She rolled a thick monster of a joint, and her wet, shiny tongue slowly licked the inside of the paper so it would wrap nicely.

      With a smile on his face and a boner in his pants, Brain passed out.

ANOTHER CHAPTER

Jack was pleased, very pleased.

Hooksville was the oasis in the middle of his tortured life. He'd been waiting for this moment, forever. Finally, he discovered the means to his destiny. Punching into a clock every day was for sheep like Brain, and he wasn't one for doing what other people wanted. To hell with following rules or laws. He was meant to get rich his way; take advantage of all the suckers, get really high while doing it and die young.

Of course, there would be women. Whores like Miko who were attracted to the smell of money. This building was perfect. Maybe he could even run it as a brothel. It would be nice if he could depend on Brain for something. Maybe the nerd could count money all day. More importantly, money had to pay for muscle, and most of his men, with their guns, could use this building as the security center. But where to set up the labs?

He wasn't disturbed nor surprised by the bum who sat huddled against the weathered aluminum siding of a building that was still largely intact. The fat, rough-looking man squatted in the dust with a pen in his hand and a notebook on his lap, dreamily scribbling away.

Bums were going to be a problem. They must have figured this place would be safe, and maybe they were the local ghosts who scared people away. They would have to be exterminated like an unwelcome infestation of rats.

Jack would have no choice but to beat the shit out of him—just close enough to death—so he would scamper away and warn his friends that Hooksville was off limits. But no, that wouldn't do at all. He would have to kill him outright to keep him from talking.

"Whatcha up to, partner?" Jack hooked his thumbs into his belt loops and kicked up dust. The bum smelled like piss and olive oil. "Drawing a pretty picture?"

The bum nodded. "You came here to see the comic store," he croaked.

Jack smirked. "I happen to be a big fan of Superman, myself."

Grinding his teeth, the bum emitted a low growl and furrowed his eyebrows. His pen scratched away furiously on the paper, his gaze never leaving Jack.

"It's right here," the man said. "The place you want to see. You know the owner skinned people alive and hung their flesh up on the walls like wallpaper? Covered the windows with it. So I heard."

Jack nodded. "And they never caught him, right?" He could feel the familiar edge scraping against his fragile mood. He tightly clenched his fists, cracking his knuckles into his palms because he regretted leaving his Vicodin in the van. His nose started to itch, and the sun was finally getting to him.

"Go on in and take a look." The man nodded to a building that was still in decent shape, untouched by fire or vandalism. "It's what you came for, i'dnit?"

Now was the time to take care of the bum. The crusty dude kept staring at him while scratching away with the pen. There was no other sound save for that pen, moving at the speed of light over the page.

"Just take a peek inside," the bum suggested. "You can see the front windows from out here. Don't even have to go in. Satisfy your curiosity, and you can tell all yer buddies you saw it for yerself."

Heat raced around his earlobes, and his ears were filled with a terrible ringing. He blinked furiously and felt his heart race while sweat slid along the back of his neck to yellow his shirt collar. If he could just get back to the van it would be so much easier to deal with all this. An hour passed since his last Vicodin. Any minute now, the headache would start pounding away.

"Fuck it," Jack gritted his teeth and peered into the open doorway into a room of shadow.

The ringing in his ears grew louder as his eyes struggled to adjust in the dark. He kept staring into the old comic store. He felt light-headed and wanted to lie down in the sun. Let it cook him right there, but he continued to stare. His heart hammered away. His ears burned. The rank smell of the piss-soaked bum and his blanket wasn't enough to make him turn away. He took a step forward and lingered on the threshold, a border between absolute darkness and scorching sunlight.

Jack stood at the foot of a mountain, staring up into bleak, gray clouds that charged impossibly fast over the sky. He was cold. Snowflakes slowly drifted down from the stormy heaven. He hugged himself for warmth and watched the time pass him by, faster than he could keep up with it. Clouds didn't move that quickly, but time did, unless he could freeze it and hold it in the palm of

31

his hands. If he could just stop it long enough so he could get himself situated and set everything up. He had so many plans, so many ideas, and it was all just a matter of...

Time.

He flicked his tongue out and snagged a snowflake in midair. His tongue became immediately numb.

Pure cocaine, falling to the earth from above.

With his body shuddering from the ecstasy, Jack cupped his hands together like he did when he used to receive the host wafer that represented Christ when he was a boy at mass. Cocaine dropped into his gullet while it collected in his hands.

He buried his face in his palms and breathed the snowpile straight to his brain. Warmth flooded his head.

Everything started to shake at once. The ground beneath his feet trembled, and he fought to keep his balance while the wonderful drug floated around his head, slipping over his cold, bare forearms and blanketing his hair. By keeping his balance, he could keep getting high. He needed to stay upright to fill his head. There was more and more of it falling around him, but the world wouldn't stop shuddering.

He saw it then, and couldn't believe his eyes.

An avalanche of cocaine sliding down the mountain toward him. He knew it was cocaine: what else could it be? He was dreaming, and in his dream he was wrecked out of his mind. It was the perfect world for him, and in his own fantasy he could die happily, with a

32

smile on his face.

He stretched out his hands and thought he heard an orchestra playing in his head. Yes, let the angels sing, because he deserved to die this way. Soon, the entire world would be his and this is what it would feel like. Complete control over a dream, the king of the universe.

The avalanche stopped suddenly at the foot of the mountain, inches away from him as if someone hit the pause button on the remote control. The quaking stopped, and so did the snow. He wasn't cold anymore, but suddenly very hot.

Blood from his nose slipped over his upper lip. His hands trembled uncontrollably while it felt like someone drove a needle straight into his heart. The pain in his chest made it difficult to breathe.

Something moved within the hills and valleys of the avalanche that stopped in front of him. Jack inhaled deeply and smelled the coke, which ignited his heart anew with the flurry of beats that usually precluded the feeling of butterflies floating around in the stomach right before you call a girl you actually like. Jack could never describe what cocaine smelled like—it was simply its own smell, pure and beautiful, a thing unique unto itself and wholly wonderful.

Miles of cocaine lay before him and strange shifts within the glittering, pure white horizon reminded him of moles tunneling beneath the dirt. It was all his for the taking, just like the world. It opened itself up to him like any other scrawny crack-whore who needed him for the promise of euphoria he gave unto them, each damned soul alike licking his fingers like loyal dogs.

Piles of coke exploded as large, fleshy shapes emerged. Jack froze where he stood and looked upon the towering beasts who snorted and oinked, their wet snouts protruding over pink, grotesque bodies. Each wore a police vest and had man-like hands which held an assortment of guns; a shotgun, a machine gun, or a handgun of some sort.

They were the pigs. The pigs had found him, after all this time.

Each time he got behind the wheel of his car, he searched his rearview mirror for them. Every car, every cautious shopper in a store, was affiliated somehow with the pigs. They were everywhere, and they were always watching, waiting for him to make a mistake. They snorted and wrinkled their snouts at him. Even now, he wouldn't plead or beg.

From both fists, he saluted their dedication with a middle finger.

Bursts of light exploded in front of his eyes, and their pig faces and pig bodies disappeared behind the glare. Somewhere, fireworks were going off. Big ones. His body shook, and he lost all feeling in his arms and legs. Something wet splashed him in the face. He felt himself being lifted from the ground by a powerful force. Suspended in the air, he continued to shake while the fireworks exploded all around him, filling his world full of pain that overcame the coke he'd just ingested.

They shot him. Over and over again, they shot him. He felt bullets exit his body, and he withstood every one of them. He was still alive. They could never kill him. The pigs would never win.

He watched as his tattered left arm was separated from the shoulder. He realized he was screaming against the waves of pain. He looked down to find his legs had burst in clouds of blood and gore, and his other arm was soon gone, too. He could still hear the pigs, snorting and oinking through the fireworks.

Mommy had left on the Fourth of July one year. She left and told him to enjoy the fireworks. Her eyelashes were curled, and she wore her best dress. Her hair was sprayed and straightened. She seemed incredibly sad, and before she left, she paused on the porch and looked back at him. She was about to say something and then didn't. He never saw her again save in the realm of dreams when he laid his head down to rest in the orphanage that dragged him off the street.

His entire body was finally gone, shredded unto nothing. His body had been committed to oblivion, and his eyeballs dissolved in the mess of violence. He could still smell and hear. He could still feel the pain.

Even without his eyes, Jack saw a piece of his face lying against rocks that were strewn in front of the cocaine avalanche. The glorious snow was colored in shades of pink and red from his death. An ear lay on one rock, and on the other, his cell phone remained intact. It vibrated, and on the screen he could see a name. He tried to look closer through the haze of pain. It read—

"Somewhere… Over the Rain-bow…"

"… anyway, Doc, that's the song I get in my head when I think about that particular incident. And I'm not even a big Judy Garland fan or anything. Didn't watch *Wizard of Oz* more than a couple times."

"Interesting. Brian, I need to ask you something because I've noticed a pattern in your speech. You often refer to yourself as Brain rather than Brian. You explained to me that Jack gave you this nickname and it stuck to you, that it followed you everywhere you went and you hated it, but you talk in the third person, or the first person… can you elaborate?"

"Well, I have Brain powers. I thought it was obvious. I mean, that's my name. No. On my birth certificate it says Brian Powers. You know, even my mom used to call me Brain after a while. I wrote it on a job application once. I'm not confused or anything. Or maybe. I don't know. You're the one to ask. Am I confused?"

"Do you want me to call you Brain?"

"I thought you were going to ask me about my mother. We've been sitting here now for… I mean, look, isn't that where it all starts? You ask about my mother and then you break me down into tears. I was expecting that."

"Are you Brain of Brian?"

"I've always been good with numbers. Nothing has changed. Have you ever seen *Rain Man?*"

"Brain, I want you to tell me what happened next. In your story, you have Jack dying in his dream where he realizes his worst... fears. Is that correct? I'm trying to keep track, and please correct me if I'm wrong, but it says here that Damien Shears draws people with a pen given to him by the aliens. When he draws people with the pen they retreat into a dream-state where they experience their worst fears, while in the real world, Shears skins them and decorates his walls with their skin. And the aliens... let me just make sure I'm correct... the aliens want data about the human condition so they can learn how to conquer us, and they thought Damien was the best candidate... they protect the town of... Hookersville... no, sorry, Hooksville... so nobody can come there. Nobody can see it on satellite. But it's on the maps."

"Are you... uh... hmm..."

"..."

"Listen Doc, you got it right. That's the story. I think it's realistic enough. It's no more outlandish than a Batman story. I mean, if you think about Spider Man, he has his spidey-sense and he knows when danger's coming, right? He can dodge attacks, and he can climb walls... Batman is nothing more than a depressed millionaire who knows martial arts and has a lot of money. I guess if you taught Bill Gates kung-fu he could become Batman, too. Maybe he is and we just don't know it."

"Brain or Brian?"

"Jack wasn't dead. That's one twist in the story. You would think he's dead, that Damien killed him, but he had something else in mind. Have you ever seen the movie *Inception?* Actually, they did a really good spoof on the movie on *South Park*... do you watch it? Listen, let me tell you, Doc, I woke up and realized some bad shit was going down. I mean, Jack was crazy. I knew that."

"Yes. Continue, please."

OR SOMETHING ELSE LIKE IT
SOMEWHERE ELSE

Brain woke with a start; he quickly sat up as the van doors opened to reveal eye-piercing white light. He was alone in the van, and he peeled his sticky arms off the shaggy purple rug. His first thought was how Kirk's bad taste in decoration mirrored his bad taste in women. His second thought was how Kirk's bad taste in women mirrored his bad taste in cars. His third thought was that Kirk was a loser.

Someone hopped onto the rear bumper. Brain could see an outline against the sunlight, and while he squinted his eyes, he crawled through the van and plopped onto the bumper to find himself sitting next to Jack.

The sun was starting to slip into the clouds, its fierce orange glow indicating that sunset was approaching. Jack didn't look at him, but methodically bent his head low and cupped his hand over the cigarette in his mouth while struggling to light it, even though there wasn't any wind.

Brain's mouth was parched, and he was fighting the lingering effects of a hangover. It didn't take much to get him drunk, though its power over him was intensified when joined with the heat of an Arizona sun.

Jack still didn't acknowledge him when he took his first drag, the menthol smell sticking to the air. He watched Jack's hands fall to his lap, and he wondered why his over-anxious friend was in such a calm state of mind. There was something wrong with Jack's hands… he stared hard at Jack's long fingers and saw red crusted beneath the fingernails and staining his knuckles.

"Shit," Jack said casually. "Hot as balls."

"It's late," Brain remarked groggily. "Where's all our water? Did Kirk and Jamie take it?"

Jack shrugged, still not looking at him.

"Where are they?"

"Fuck do I know?" Jack replied. "I don't know where people go when they die. Anyway, I chopped them up. The sun was getting to me. And we're out of pills. Thanks to Kirk and his slutty girlfriend."

"Um… you…"

"We're not going to argue about this, are we?" Jack's irritation was evident. His fingers were trembling, and Brain knew from experience they were cold and clammy to the touch.

Brain was at a loss for words. Jack had to be kidding, but the stains on his hands were incredibly odd. Nothing was beyond his friend, of course. If enough time elapsed since his last fix, who knew to what extreme he might go? The whole drive through the desert had been strange—maybe this was the *real* master plan. Maybe Jack had finally gone over the edge and all he wanted to do was kill people.

"Dude," Jack chuckled, "you should have seen her face when Kirk's head popped off. Oh man, it was so *fucking funny!* She started shaking and crying, I mean blubbering like an idiot. Couldn't understand a word she said. Oh man, she pissed herself… dude, you should have been there. You missed out."

"I was asleep," was all Brain could think to say.

"I'm glad I found the axe when I did. The pocket knife wasn't going to get the job done. Would've been a mess. Anyway, so his head just kind of rolled. He was dead anyway, by that point. I don't know if it was blood loss or shock, but I managed to get both his arms off right at the shoulders, and his legs at the knee caps."

"An axe?"

"Well, I figured I'd get a better kick out of it if Jamie watched Kirk get cut. She just stood there, man, didn't even try to run. So I just nailed her right in the stomach. She had a surprised look on her face. She fell and kind of lay there and moaned for a bit. I let her die slowly. I know that sounds kind of shitty, but I started to get hard while she moaned. Ain't that weird?"

"I didn't really know Jamie that well," Brian said as if they were discussing the weather. "Didn't you go out with her for a while?"

"No, but she spent the night a few times. Even when her and Kirk were together… dude was so strung out he couldn't take care of her. Anyway, while Jamie was on the ground moaning… well, I didn't know what else to do. I just whipped it out and jerked it. Just jerked it right over her. Covered her in it. She was still alive."

Jack continued to smoke his cigarette while watching the sun's light wither and die over the expired town.

Brain could think of only one question to ask, even when so many others might be more obvious. "Have you seen Miko?"

Jack's eyebrows darted up. "Who's Miko? Someone from one of those Jap comics you read? Is that a character from a comic you were drawing back in school? Shit. I almost remember…"

Fumbling nervously with his fingers, Brain became very confused. He knew it was stupid to drink and drive, and in the first place it was just stupid to drink. Jack and company had their drugs and their fun, but Brain was a working stiff who woke up at the same time every morning and went to bed watching Cartoon Network. Weakening his perception played deadly tricks with his thoughts. Did he hear Jack say he murdered Jamie and Kirk?

"Anyway," Jack said, "I figured you'd know you're supposed to die next. You're as good as dead without me. I've always protected you, helped you, given you a reason to live. The way I see it, you *owe* me your life. You would have killed yourself by now if it weren't for me."

Brain stared into the dust at his feet and realized how right Jack was. As always, everything he said was correct; Jack could never be wrong.

"I don't see a problem with it," Brain announced.

"Excellent," Jack slowly turned his squared–jawed face, his eyebrows furrowing deeply while a cloud of smoke obscured his deep, brown eyes.

"I Know Dream Sequences Are Anti-Climactic…"

"There's nothing wrong with them."

"That doesn't help, Doc."

"Brain, there's a lot of symbolic value to dreams, but you already know that, or else you wouldn't have included it."

"Jack has been such a huge part of my life. I always thought he wanted good things for me, but he used me. I knew that all along. I never forgot it. I don't know why I thought he brought Miko for me."

"That's still bothering you. Would you like to discuss it further?"

"I obey the rules and do everything right. I didn't feel pressure to lose my virginity. Women have scared me for so long they were like a different species, an animal I wasn't supposed to eat for dinner."

"I see Miko is still a sensitive subject. Why don't we change topics? What's the first thing that comes to mind when I ask you to picture your mother?"

"When I woke up, I was covered in puke, and I wasn't sure it was mine."

TRACK 4: THINGS THAT CAN SLEEP FOR ONE MILLION DOLLARS, PLEASE

As far as bums went, the guy at the comic book store had to be among the coolest. Sure, he smelled like sewage and diarrhea, but as long as you stayed ten feet away from him, his personality shone through his dirt-caked face.

"So this is the place!" Jamie giggled and hopped on one foot while scanning the walls and windows.

"Yeah, man!" Kirk stomped on the dusty floorboards. "Shit. *Look at this place*. People were actually killed here. Their skin was hung up right there"—he pointed to a window—"and all over that wall. The whole place was covered!"

"It's amazing," Jamie's voice betrayed awe and excitement. She was standing in a place made infamous by time and murder. It was like being in a haunted house with your friends and emerging as the only one who wasn't afraid.

The bum lit the last of the candles and blew out his match. "This is the place," he said gruffly.

After showing up at the church by scaring the shit out of them, the bum managed to stay Kirk's drunken wrath by showing him a bunch of pictures. They were artistic renditions of people, beautiful portraits carefully shaded in pen. The bum was pretty good, and he offered them a tour of the town and a visit

44

to the comic store if they would pose for him so he could add to his collection of drawings. One of the pictures looked like Jack.

"So you live here?" Kirk shook his head while holding his guitar by its neck. "Damn man, that's creepy. I guess I could see why though, I mean, it's not like anyone comes around to bother you. I bet there's a bunch of bums living here."

"Nope," the hobo said. "Just me."

Jamie was responsible for the last bit of whiskey. She held the bottle in her fist, and she drunkenly swayed on her feet in the dark, stuffy comic store. As long as Kirk was around, she wasn't afraid of anything. Kirk got into a lot of fights at clubs and concerts to protect her, and most people who knew better back home didn't screw around with him. She knew she was pretty. It was always fun to watch Kirk get red-faced and agitated when he caught other men looking at her, even though she was the one who smiled or winked; she might toss her hair and bat her eyelashes like only she could do. It was a turn on to see Kirk get worked up.

Once in a while, when Kirk wasn't around, Jack played with her. Jack was an asshole and didn't give a damn about her, but that's what she liked about him. There wasn't a person in the world he genuinely cared about, although he could pretend he cared better than anyone she knew. It was funny how he often led the nerd on—what was his name?—Brain. She couldn't remember his real name. Oh, well.

The trip into the desert was the perfect opportunity to sleep with both Jack and Kirk in the same night and start a huge fight between two of her favorite men. Kirk was secretly afraid of Jack. She knew because he always did whatever Jack wanted, as if he owed him his life. She had fantasies of Kirk learning about Jack but not having the balls to do a damn thing about it. Jack wouldn't keep her around, but she would throw herself at him, and he would resist. Meanwhile, Kirk would work up the courage and blow Jack's brains out and conquer her for a little while. Jack would die because of her, and Kirk would kill a man just to have her. It was perfect.

"Will you sit in the chairs?" the bum asked both of them.

"Whatever man," Kirk shrugged. "I don't really care about your pictures, to be honest. I'm here to party, and you smell like an unwashed dick that skull-fucked an old lady's corpse five years ago. I got my buzz on man, I don't feel like sitting. I'm out here looking for a ghost. You seen him? You know what I'm talking about?"

The rage was starting to take hold of Kirk. Jamie could see his shoulders tense and his eyes growing wider. Both of them had a high tolerance for chemicals; their bodies were saturated and practically kept upright by pills and booze, so they could party all night long. Kirk had already decided he was going to include the bum in his plans.

The bum didn't seem impressed. "What if I told you I'm him?"

He came around the counter of the old store, a mountain of a man wearing a strange outfit made of

46

leathery patches that were different shades of red and brown. His shaved head and unwashed face made him seem a penitent monk who'd decided to take a pilgrimage to a garbage dump to find the Fountain of Youth.

"You're the killer?" Kirk squared his shoulders. It was almost time.

"I was here when it happened." The bum nodded slowly. "I saw it all, and I can tell you about it. You would love the story."

"Ooooh." Jamie rubbed her thin arms in mock fear. "I like scary stories."

Kirk was silent for a long time, staring down the bum while candlelight swayed to a silent beat, the sunset's desperate rays painting the grimy windows in russet-shaded vomit.

"I used to come here when I was a kid," Kirk said thoughtfully. "Loved comic books. Used to get a hard-on for Black Cat. It was the owner who killed some people in here, and I don't remember you being here. Dude would be old and crusty by now... you're saying you killed people in here? Man, that's some radical shit. I'm down for hearing *that* story."

Jamie clapped her hands, and Kirk hollered like a wounded wolf or a choking cat.

"I'm a celebrity," the bum said. "Yes, I killed people. I didn't want to be a legend or anything, you know. I just wanted to be an artist. Like you. You must like music."

"Yeah," Kirk brushed his hair out of his eyes. "I dig the classics, you know. Skynnyrd, Zeppelin, Floyd, all that, man. That's my shit. We gotta bring the classics back, some real music with poetry, some guitars and drums… real music by real musicians. I can melt some faces with my guitar man, like Page and Hendrix."

"Let me tell you a story," the bum said. "Let me tell you about art and murder. I have the answers to some of our most important questions, if only you'll listen. Sit down and let me draw you both while I speak. My art is all I have."

"I dig that." Kirk pulled up one of the wooden chairs across the dusty floor, and Jamie did the same. Kirk looked around at the empty shelves as if seeing them for the first time. "Bought a lot of comics here. Yeah man… a lot of comics."

"Great," the bum cut him off, unimpressed with the fanboy flashbacks. "Sit still, and let my pen draw the beauty I see but can't put into words. My story, you see, it begins…"

.... In My Bedroom...

"...where I often sat and dreamed. The store was doing quite well, and I had Mother to thank for that. I didn't want to own a store. I was an artist. I was better than all those hacks who draw nothing but boobs and guns. The last thing I wanted was to sell their books and their stupid stories. Mother had a plan for me even though it wasn't exactly HER plan! I was sitting in my room, drawing away, when I realized I was too good for the world. Too talented, too perfect. There was something missing in my life, and the next day would be the turning point I needed.

"Let me go back in time a bit, to a time of dinosaurs and fast women.

"My mother was an artist too, you see. A woman with a unique vision that couldn't be appreciated by the simpletons and the fools, something you can understand, I'm sure. She was ahead of her time, but despite all her best efforts, she couldn't get off the ground. She couldn't work menial jobs while suffering the depression that any starving artist submits to. She worked hard for nothing.

"When she was still a young lass in high school, she wanted to do so many things with her skills! Design clothes and costume jewelry, set design, photography, painting... nothing was out of her reach. She was being courted by other artists, and she was praised as the second coming of Van Gogh and Coco Chanel. A lady

49

of privilege, her fate as an Ivy League graduate had already been determined the day she was born, but her skills would be showcased at universities around the world, and then her art would take her beyond the stars.

"She was abducted by aliens. The story of what happened to her while she was in their clutches will never be known. When they returned her to Earth, she ran away from home. Her story was a tragic one, but after two days there were no more headlines and only her parents wanted her back. The fashion world blamed it on madness caused by such a profound mind. Most people thought she was dead on the side of a road somewhere.

"She ran as far and as fast as she could from her talents, drifting across the country,. Her imagination haunted her fragile mind, and she did everything a degenerate could do to make money on the road. Lonely and wasted, she struggled to survive; she was too much of a coward to kill herself, though she tried once.

"Her alien friends intervened.

"They returned to her because she was precious; they managed to probe the depths of her consciousness to derive the secrets of human suffering in an attempt to discover the idea of 'soul.' The aliens are immortal, and they fear the idea of death. It's been their mission to discover if an afterlife exists.

"As for my Mommy Dearest, seven years had passed since her escape from civilized life. She was barely alive, dragging her druggie, STD-carrying body into the West, where she was finally knocked up. She was never sure who Daddy was.

"The aliens had driven her to the brink of madness, and they had been providing cash to make sure she could feed her drug habits. They were intrigued by the idea that drugs could open her mind to greater feats of the imagination. With a baby in her belly, they realized a new opportunity and decided they would do all they could to keep her healthy. They abducted her again and cleaned the poison out of her system.

"She was hardly born-again. She'd been living on the road for a long time, and her abilities suffered for it. Everything she created seemed borne out of a nightmare, and most of her work was destroyed while she moved around. Her identity had been buried long ago, but the beast inside her demanded the blood sacrifice only an artist can provide.

"I know what you're thinking: Why didn't she just contact her old friends in the art industry? Why didn't she come back home? It wasn't that easy, because her art had suffered. It had become distorted, something unreal and shapeless. A scream trapped in a soundproof room.

"The aliens purged the shit from her body and watched her struggle with menial jobs. She had to make ends meet, of course. She had a baby on the way, and her friends wouldn't let her escape life. She was trapped in this world with the mind that was always on fire, raging with ideas shaped by torment and nightmare.

"After I was born the aliens had already given up on her. A lot of men roamed through my life, in and out of the house, half-drunk and mad with lust. They beat my poor mother and threw money in her face. I knew what sex was at an early age. I flipped through books on the floor of our shabby apartment's living room because we couldn't afford cable, and on the couch she wriggled and panted beneath a fat, bald man.

"Sure, I had a troubled life, but I'm not complaining. I mean, YOU might call it troubling, but I think it was fun beating the crap out of snot-nosed nerds and stealing their lunch money and comic books. I was a big kid, and I knew to get what I wanted I had to fight for every scrap, so fight I did. It was a means of survival too, but hey, that's how I discovered the Marvel universe! And DC, which is far superior. There were so many imitators, so many upstarts… but I'm getting ahead of myself. You want to hear about aliens and murder.

"Beating up kids and reading comics proved to be excellent distractions from my mother's whoring and drinking. She often disappeared for nights on end without so much as a phone call, and I had to fend for myself. At twelve years old with a bottle of beer in my fist (it's easy to get alcohol when you live in the ghetto, but I'm stating the obvious, right? Nod your heads but don't nod off, not yet, even though I know you're getting sleepy, though you should understand I want to keep on talking. Yes, yes I do want to keep talking, and when I'm finished with my story and ONLY when I'm finished you can sleep, because then my pictures will be almost done, and we can finish them, yes, we can finish them for all time)… I drunkenly trashed our bedroom (we slept together because there was only the one bedroom, and I had always been in her bed when I was

52

baby because she couldn't buy a crib, and so, yes, I slept in the same bed as my mother). I opened up her condoms and vibrators and chains and threw her bras and cheap Wal-Mart makeup against the wall until I made a discovery.

"Her scribblings. Her drawings. Her vain attempts to rediscover sanity.

"It was like slipping on an oil spill. I mean, it's sticky and awful, it smells, and it's black. It reflects nothing but darkness and swallows any darkness that attempts to penetrate THAT darkness. It must have been what it felt like the first time a young man discovers porn while he's all alone at home. Maybe I drooled. The pictures shook in my hands, and I kept flipping through them, over and over again. I couldn't stop looking at them. It was like being introduced to a stranger who was supposed to be your blind date only you discovered she was the perfect woman and she was already married or otherwise impossible to obtain. Maybe that's a little too complicated. How about this? I was disturbed and amazed at the same time. Or maybe that's a bit too confusing…

"I can't describe her pictures to you, because your minds can't comprehend such majesty. Her work belongs to another world, or at least, another universe. I was inspired. I never confronted her because she earned my respect.

"Drawing my own comics became my second-favorite pastime after pummeling my classmates. I had a gift for art, like my mother, and I finally had something to do while sitting in class. I'd read all the comics I could steal. Back in those days, you'd find comics at the grocery store and at 7-11. Teachers didn't give a damn what I did as long as I didn't break any arms in class. I had a reputation, and I did all I could to live up to it. Most of the kids in the school cowered in fear in my presence, and I didn't need a group of followers to help me out or validate my need for violence and power.

"I stayed in school long enough to graduate because it was a good source of income and pleasure. When I came home one evening, Mother wanted to talk to me, something she rarely did. She explained to me that we were moving into a house in a small town, and I was going to have money to buy out the owner of a comic book store. The town, as you well know, is Hooksville.

"My whole life was laid out for me!

"I slapped her across the face. I slapped her twice, actually. I punched her in the gut and watched her double over at me feet, puking up chunks of chicken from her Campbell's chicken noodle soup dinner. I never had her at my mercy before, and the power surging through me filled me with pleasure. I threw her onto the couch and ripped her clothes off while she whimpered and coughed through her snot-covered lips. I called her all the names I wanted to call her and slapped her across the face two more times, cracking open her bottom lip and spilling blood. I loved seeing the way her thin blond hair swept over her face when her head rocked sideways with each blow. There was a moment, for just a second there… while my mother blinked her eyes at me through strands of hair, I felt… adoration. Love. It was an uncomfortable feeling, like a bowel movement that wouldn't be freed.

"I took off for a walk outside, leaving her on the couch to rot. I could smell the garbage from the dump across the street from out apartment building, a place I used to hang out and hide in the dark to be alone with my thoughts.

"The money wasn't an issue. I assumed she'd been stashing for years and saved up some money, but why did she have a specific plan?

"A loud humming sound throbbed in my ears and sharp pain in my head sent me to my knees in the dirt. I shut my eyes against the agony, and when I opened them, I found myself surrounded by walls that bled. I was trapped in a trembling room composed of bone and flesh that melted and sizzled. It seemed a never-ending flood of blood that oozed over the long bones.

"More than anything I just wanted to get off my knees, but I slipped through the liquid mess. My hands were covered in gore. I fell on my face and could taste the coppery syrup on my lips. I wasn't afraid of anything, and here I was, confused by my hallucination. I didn't suffer from blackouts or any bad dreams, so what the hell was going on?

"Their voices called out to me. I heard them, a nagging series of noises that pulsed through the bloody room.

"*Molb, molb, molb, molb, molb, molb, molb…*

"That's the noise. They kept doing it: *molb, molb, molb, molb…*

"You want to know what they look like? I can't tell you that. But I will say they told me everything, and explained I must take the comic store. I was destined for greatness, and I would help them with their grand experiment. They would protect me. They wanted me to experience my wildest fantasies without fear of punishment. All I had to do was say yes.

"Let me skip ahead to the fun part. We moved out, and I took over the comic store. You know my store, but you don't know what I was up to. I realized the potential of my gift. I was an amazing artist, but the aliens wanted me to kill people. That's really what it comes down to. They figured they would give me a tryout before sending me up to the big leagues, and I enjoy feeling powerful. You know… chopping people up and hanging their limbs over my bathtub and letting the blood drip onto my hairy chest. I like swirling the blood over my nipples. I liked to wrap intestines around my neck and shoulders and dance in front of the mirror and pretend to be Alice Cooper.

"I'm glad this doesn't repulse you. I can tell you're good people.

"Killing is just something I like to do. Kind of like brushing your teeth, and I've done *that* with bone marrow for toothpaste. My alien friends did all kinds of cool things to throw the authorities off my scent, and usually I buried the bodies in my backyard, or what was left of them. We had a wood-burning stove in the basement, which might sound strange if you live in Arizona, but it had its uses.

"Mommy Dearest used to sit and watch me

chop people up, and she would have her pen and paper on her lap and she would scribble away. She never shared her life story with me. I learned about her past from my alien friends. I never acted surprised the first time she sat there and doodled while I hacked away. She drew with the same pen, this same pen I'm using right now.

"The store was doing pretty well until my mother finally became a raving lunatic. She would make the *molb molb molb* sounds in her sleep, and then she began sleep*walking,* if you can believe that. She would sit watching TV all day until I brought home a new playmate. She stopped whoring when we moved because she was inspired by my new hobby. I became her caretaker, and I really got sick of it because I had better things to do than give her baths and wash her underwear. She was an invalid, and I didn't feel bad when I had her dragged off to the nuthouse.

"After she was gone the aliens visited me again. They were pretty upset by my decision but they understood. All they really cared about was her pen, which they made especially for her. They explained why it was so special, and I finally put the puzzle pieces together.

"One day I was standing around in the store, and I was doodling on the counter. I was drawing a picture of the store and everyone in it. After a while, they all fell asleep. I closed up shop for the day and chopped everyone up. My weapon of choice was an axe and a pair of scissors. The axe was in the backroom, but I had a hard time finding the scissors. After I made a mess I cut up strips of their skin and hung it over the windows. I wanted to redecorate for a while, and I figured it was my best chance to get it done.

"The aliens protect me. They always have and always will. I'm invincible!

"Dammit! It happened again! My audience sleeps. I wasn't finished with my story! Whatever. Fuck it."

SKIP, SKIP, SKIP, STOP. PLAY. SKIP, SKIP, STOP. GET A NEW DISC... THIS ONE HAS SCRATCHES ON IT AND A FEW FINGERPRINTS. SEE?

At last, he was a star.

With the electric guitar pressed tightly against his abs while he gyrated his leather-clad crotch to the squealing instrument's crescendo, time seemed to slow down. He watched his fingers betray the genius of his craft, the artistry of each movement masterfully plucking away, moving across the neck of his phallic extension. He glanced up at the crowded amphitheater, the thousands of upturned, sweaty faces flush with beer and marijuana and fantasies that one day, they would be on the stage like him, or in another lifetime they *were* him.

His shape passed through shifting color as a rainbow of spotlights accentuated his demigod status, an object worthy of worship and desire, of wisdom and inspiration, perfection and wonder. This was Kirk's moment, the guitar the majestic presence filling the ears, minds, and hearts of the fleshy blob, the fist-pumping, clapping fanboys, the teenage girls who fingered themselves while huge, life-sized posters of his presence hugged pink bedroom walls, the sneering critics who cried when his guitar warbled in the likeness of the legends who'd been buried in the garbage pile of TOP 40 HITS. The Fender Stratocaster was his almighty hammer as he ascended into the pantheon of immortals,

59

smashing his weapon down upon the floor to unleash the power of music.

While his hand slid through spectrums of sound and glory, he threw his head back and looked upon the writhing mass of flesh clothed in darkness. They screamed his name, though he couldn't hear them. He saw it in the ears that glowed, the mouths that moved; he felt it in the vibrating stage beneath his combat boots. They wanted him. They needed him. He awakened a primal lust which slept in their souls. They wanted to fuck everything and drown in an ocean of sweat and beer.

Crowd surfers cruised across the sea of hands. For a moment, while his fingers raped the chords in rhapsodic measurements of harmony, he remembered what it was like to crowd surf. He remembered what it was like to have a hot chick pass through his hands and how great it was to grab at anything he could without fear of penalty. He never thought he would experience so much power, so much freedom, in his life. He was wrong. There was nothing greater than being a rock star.

Light passed over a familiar face in the front of the crowd. Kirk's heart skipped a beat, and he nearly lost the tonal essence of the soaring tribute to his own musical prowess. He brushed locks of hair away from his eyes while he moved deftly across the front of the stage. He'd seen his share of women's breasts popping out at him for his eyes to devour, but something with a hint of nagging familiarity summoned his eyes back to the crowd. He searched distractedly while his fingers slowed. Time ebbed, a frail thing in the midst of musical prowess, the guitar's motherfucking-superpower-overload burning through warm skulls.

Peering through the darkness, a face glowed against the backdrop of coalescing meat. Slicked hair and narrow eyes, a cigarette dangling between his lips—even though it was illegal to smoke in the amphitheater. A smirk touched the corners of his mouth.

Kirk mouthed the name of his junk-man, his devil, his lifeline to a realm of scattered promises and needs.

Jack. Jack was watching. Jack was always watching. Jack's cold handshake, Jack's wet eyes, Jack's calm, smooth voice. Why would he be here? Always waiting for Jack, always needing Jack. Was Jack pleased with his music? Was Jack going to judge him, criticize him? Was Jack going to tell the press he was the man who fed Kirk's soul? Jack wanted money or else he wouldn't be 'wasting time' at a concert. Jack only went places if there was a purpose, an opportunity.

The house lights went up, and the illusion of grandiose ascension over man was shattered. Kirk kept playing; it was all he knew to do. Something was wrong, but nobody was cutting the power to the instruments. The show must go on, and it would. The crowd was a swirling mass of worms, slipping and wriggling against each other, their mouths open to the ceiling like expectant baby birds. Kirk could smell the human mixture of spectator stink. The combination of beer, vomit, and sweat smelled like the minutes after summer sex. Wet and anxious, the light revealed a joyous species.

The drumbeat had disappeared, the bass line was gone. Kirk glanced over his shoulders and found his band mates had left him alone on the stage. The fog of war and grease lifting over the stage, the vaporous after-birth of the million-dollar show. His fingers stopped playing, yet the guitar still warbled. For a moment, Kirk feared his entire performance was nothing more than a recording and he'd been lip-synching, but that wasn't right. That hadn't been happening at all.

The Stratocaster vibrated against his hips. He helplessly spread out his arms as if the instrument were an endangered animal over whose corpse he stood and asked for blame and suspicion to disappear. Smoke rose from the thousands before him, and there was Jack, standing mutely with his cigarette smoldering between his lips.

Kirk couldn't move. He was at the mercy of the music and the crowd. He watched as flesh melted away from their bones. Blood, skin, and hair sloughed away like snot slipping through the nose of a toddler uncontested. The bodies stood as cloth and gore burned and sizzled, cooked by the powerful music that cried over the ocean of blood which flooded the amphitheater's floor. Pennies melting in a barbecue pit.

Through it all, there was Jack. Unmoved, forever unsatisfied by the world around him. He was the one who owned it, and Kirk usurped the throne.

The musician collapsed to his knees, the guitar thrust forward as an offering. He wanted to speak but his words were drowned out by the collective sigh of the melting crowd and the wailing guitar. Jack's icy gaze was fixed upon him, and Kirk wanted to turn his face away from that magisterial gaze.

Roping intestines and other organs flopped out of exposed stomachs; rib cages spilled their contents while the skeletons remained upright, their jaws working with newfound angst. Eyeballs roved back and forth within their sockets and thousands of phalanges in different shapes and sizes reached for the stage. A tide of bone surged forward. Feet slid on gory entrails, wormy penises, and bushy scalps. Teeth chattered in skewed mouths. Jack stood against the railing as the mob traded its flesh for music.

They clawed at the stage and climbed over the edge, a wave of skeletons grinding their teeth and grabbing for him, wrenching the strapped guitar over his head and standing over him while he shriveled beneath their malevolent stares. They ripped the chords out of his instrument; the guitar solo continued to soar beyond his fingers and beyond his dreams.

Hot tears streamed down his cheeks. As the dead converged upon him, his last thought was that he hadn't cried since he was a little boy, and he felt relieved.

TO BE CONTINUED NEXT MONTH: THE ALIENS ARE REVEALED AT LAST!

(here is my attempt at illustrating an advertisement for next month's issue. please excuse us for our indiscretion in this matter: we are currently looking for a new artist to do pencils, because we truly want the aliens to be gruesome when you finally see them. however, at this time, we are having a hard time finding an artist who can draw the aliens as the author envisions them)

TO SMELL LIKE A DREAM

Today's the day. Jack had been promising to get her a puppy for so long, just to see her smile. Kirk was passed out somewhere in his own vomit like he always was, probably from taking too many pills Jack had given him to sell. Meanwhile, Jack gave her all the OxyContin she could snort up her nose, which was far more than Kirk could manage. Her body tingled with delight; it was such an awesome day!

Jack pulled up to the humane society and parked his black Ford Explorer in the empty parking lot; orange dust caught in the sun's glow kicked up from the tires as the brakes screeched.

"Oh my *God*," Jamie shouted joyfully. "I still don't know what puppy I want! I can't decide. Will you help me decide? Jaaaaaaaaaack?"

He popped a cigarette into his mouth and nodded at the shelter. "Hurry the fuck up. Got shit to do."

She shot out of the car and scampered in her flip flops to the door. The windows were shielded by dust and iron bars. Jamie didn't wonder for one second why there were no other cars in the parking lot—nothing that could belong to an employee.

The lobby was empty, and when Jamie called out, an echo replied. All the lights were off, but she wasn't deterred. It was completely normal for the animal shelter to be empty. They couldn't possibly be closed because this was her day. Now, she was finally going to get her second chance after Macy had drowned in her pool. It was all her fault, of course. Her parents made sure she knew it. No five-year-old girl should bring a puppy into the swimming pool; what the hell was she thinking? They taught her better! She was a big girl, and big girls didn't do stupid shit. Like drown puppies.

Her arms tingled, and she couldn't feel the sweat slipping along the edge of her neck, nor was she aware of the perspiration-soaked strands of hair that fell over her forehead. All she wanted was a puppy, and it was Jack who made it all happen. He always knew what she needed; he had a natural talent for pleasure. He taught her everything she knew about hustling, and because of him, she didn't want or need for anything.

Pretty soon, she was going to take a puppy back home to her apartment! She would clean up the place and make it presentable for her new guest; needles and paper plates would be picked off the floor and vomit stains would be scraped out of the carpet near the air conditioner. Whenever she wasn't with Jack or Kirk in the clubs or the pool halls, she would sit on her loveseat and play games on her phone all day. Those were lonely hours, but they could be a lot more fun with a puppy curled up in her lap. She already knew what she would name it.

Macy.

"You gonna look around or what?" Jack asked impatiently from behind her.

She was already ahead of him. Since she was a little girl, this had been her dream and nothing would stop her. She would steal a puppy if she needed to. A part of her wanted to tiptoe to the kennel door because it was so silent; all the puppies were probably sleeping, and she would hate to disturb them. When her fingers curled around the door handle, she squealed through clenched teeth, doing all she could not to scream for joy. Jack would find that annoying, and she didn't want to piss him off.

It didn't dawn on her that the door wasn't locked. Nothing seemed out of the ordinary. Everything was as it should be as the puppies awaited new masters. All they wanted to do was roll over onto their back and expose their bellies with their tongues rolling out of their mouths, panting, eyes wide, and paws curled.

The door groaned as it swung open to reveal a dark corridor full of empty cages.

Tentatively, Jamie stepped into the kennel, her mouth agape. Where were the puppies? What happened? She peeked into every cage as she slowly walked down the corridor; dog and cat food partially filled bowls in the cages, and the damp smell of piss and feces wafted into her nose but didn't bother her. No. What bothered her was the silence, something she *felt* for the first time.

"The puppies," she whispered. "No. Oh, no. Jack, where'd they go? They're supposed to be here. This is where they sleep. I can't hear them... Jack, I can't hear anything."

When she turned around to look for Jack, he was gone. The only sound in that corridor was that of her own heart beating inside her ears and all around her. *Thump, thump, thump.* She hadn't heard her own heartbeat since she used to push her hands up against her ears to listen. Nobody was here. Jack finally abandoned her, sick of her neediness and childish fantasies. She knew she was screwed up but it didn't matter because as long as she had Jack in her life, everything would be okay. There was always enough Jack to numb her, and for the first time in several hours, she truly knew she was alive.

Nervously pushing her jean shorts toward knees that were impossibly far away, she balled her hands into tight little fists and felt her frigid fingertips bite into her palms.

"Jack?" her voice trembled. "Hello? Is there anyone…?" she choked, unable to finish because she knew it was useless. There were no cars in the parking lot. Nobody at the reception desk. No puppies.

She couldn't leave without a puppy. And besides, Jack was probably just sitting in the car smoking a cigarette, talking on his phone and setting up more deals. His time was precious. If she walked out of there without a puppy, he would be pissed because the drive would have turned out to be a complete waste. The puppies were in the back somewhere, along with the kittens. The drugs had dulled her senses; she was too high to hear them. This was one of those moments where she had to sober up quickly in order to function like an "adult."

"Okay, it's okay," she told herself. "Cute little puppy wants to be with me. I'm here for you little puppy. That's it, yeah, okay." She unfroze her limbs and took a step forward, and then another. She steadied herself against the reeking cages and moved through the rows of darkness, a faint glow at the end of the corridor signal enough that there was an end, somewhere.

The shelter was oddly cold, even though it was over a hundred degrees outside. Jamie hugged herself and wished she wasn't wearing a spaghetti-strapped tank-top. As the silence followed her through the passage, her arms itched something fierce. She scratched furiously at her forearms until her exposed, sweat-slick thighs also needed attention.

Then she saw them. Hundreds of them, jumping through the bars and leaping onto her flesh. Tiny little black specks assembled into a dust-cloud of leaping annoyances.

Fleas. Everywhere, fleas.

There was no going back. After everything Jack had done for her; screwing her in the clubs while her boyfriend, Kirk, threw drunks into the street. Giving her Oxyies while she gave him head as he talked on his cell phone in the truck. Driving her through the desert so she could fulfill her dream. All she ever wanted was a puppy.

She kept going, clawing at her arms and legs, walking awkwardly in her sandals across urine-wet floor, her toes splashing through warm puddles. Flies buzzed around her head, joining the assault with the never-ending stream of fleas. The light ahead beckoned; there would be puppies, hidden in the back, kept safe from the muck she tramped through now. She wasn't alarmed when feces oozed through the cages and plopped into the corridor around her. She was having a bad trip, or a bad come-down. Her nose and forehead were itchy but it wasn't enough to stop her. Just keep going.

A hoarse voice filled with pain echoed along the corridor. "Jamie. Please, I hurt. You hurt me real bad. Don't you know… how much I need you?"

Metal scraping along the concrete floor filled the winding hallway of cages. She started to back up, and for a moment, she couldn't feel the fleas or the flies, and she didn't mind the puddles and crap at her feet, which squished beneath her heels. She recognized that voice, and it filled her with dread. It couldn't be. Not here, not now.

"I trusted you," the sorrowful voice continued. "You were going to be my girl when I finally made it. We were going to conquer the world together. Why did you do this to me? Why?"

He never cared enough to notice her life. He was so wrapped up in his drugs and music, so why would he care now? She told him about Macy, about her fondest wish for another puppy. She couldn't just go out and get one all by herself; it needed to be a gift, something earned, something she could treasure as a reward that provided a sense of redemption.

"Stay away from me," she muttered through lips that refused to move. "Just stay away."

"I can never let you go," the scraping was closer, and she could feel it grating against her nerves. His voice rambled on. "We set the stage on fire with our love, baby. You and me. Together. Usssssssssssssssssssssssssssssss."

70

His shadow blocked out the light at the end of the corridor, a human eclipse filled with Kirk in all his glory. It was him, sure enough. He was hunched over, and a glimpse of light revealed the heavy chains wrapped around his wrists, weighing his arms and shoulders down as he stepped heavily through light and shadow. She recognized the 'Stairway to Heaven' shirt he wore nearly every day, and his neatly-manicured hair was askew over his face, but she knew it was him. Jamie felt the same disappointment, the same need for Jack to do something about this man whom she didn't have the strength to leave.

"You're not supposed to be here!" she shouted at him. "I'm here for Macy. Did you take her? Did you do something to the puppies?"

Kirk chuckled. "Sure. I did everything I could. Come here and let me show you. You'll never have to leave. You can stay here with me forever. Be mine, and I'll forgive you… I know what you've been doing…"

She wanted to shout at him, accuse him of being a spineless man who should've been fighting for her, but her feet wanted to keep moving backward. Kirk wanted to hurt her, and maybe now Jack could beat him up for all time. The fight she always wanted would finally happen, and all she had to do was run. Run back to Jack. She would have to leave Macy, but once the fight was over she could try again.

With her feet slipping through the mess, she turned and ran from Kirk. Her limbs obeyed, but she felt as if she were running on air. Her body felt light and her steps were slow; her heartbeat pounded away, *thump,*

thump, thump, while Kirk's laughter followed her. She waved flies away from her face until a sandal slipped off her feet. To hell with it; she stopped and took the other one off. Kirk wanted to hurt her; he was in one of his moods, although he was always careful not to hit her face. Always her stomach. She had never run from him before, never actually resisted him, and if he caught her it might be far worse. No matter what, she had to get away.

She shouldn't have stopped. Her bones locked up again. She was out of breath, and she felt the fleas all over her exposed skin. They slipped down her shirt and tickled her stomach and chest while flies landed on her curling toes and sweaty thighs. It would be so easy to give up and let him have his way, especially if she was going to make it worse by running. He would get her eventually.

"Be with me forever. Please, Jamie. Love me like I love you."

Time to go. She wasn't afraid. Not anymore. Adrenaline and confidence surged through her system. Her heartbeat disappeared, and her burning lungs were numb. She slipped over all manner of animal waste but she managed to steady herself between the rows of cages on either side. She ran and ran. Steel on the concrete. Laughter. No matter how much she ran she could still hear him.

A white beam of light beckoned. The corridor seemed endless but still she ran. Kirk could never have her. Jack was going to protect her. Her life was going to change, finally. Freedom was close, at last.

72

Her feet slipping and sliding, she breathlessly approached the light. Her strength failed her completely and she leaned against a wall of cages, panting and scratching. Until now, she didn't know she'd been crying.

The end of the corridor was nothing more than a ledge that opened up to a wide, blue sky. The ground had completely disappeared. She tried to shake it from her vision; she rubbed her eyes and whimpered, frustrated with her fear and the lack of escape. Nothing had gone right. What was supposed to be the best day of her life turned into a nightmare. Where was Jack? Where was the reception desk?

Beneath the ledge was a large swimming pool, one that looked just like the one at her house before her parents divorced and the house was sold. That was *her* swimming pool down there, and it wasn't too far away. She could make the jump and be okay. It was the only way out.

"Love me forever," Kirk chided her from the darkness. "I want to forgive you. Come here and give me a kiss."

There was only one way out. Without a second thought, she closed her eyes and leapt off the ledge.

Impact with the water should have been nearly instantaneous. She felt the wind on her face, but no water. She opened her eyes and realized she was still falling; she nearly choked on her heartbeat when she realized the water beneath her wasn't water at all, but a writhing mass of brown fur. Suspended in free-fall, she heard the yelping and whining of puppies, a million

73

short barks and growls, puppies climbing over each other, each one identical, a little brown hound dog with a red collar around its throat, each one the same, each one with big brown eyes and floppy ears, each one crying or panting, tongues rolling over teeth, each one Macy. Macy, Macy, everywhere.

Jamie slammed onto the bed of puppies and let their wet, sandpaper tongues lick her all over. She sighed and stared up at the bright blue sky. Everything was perfect. She belonged with Macy and had found her. Fresh tears flooded her eyes, blurring her vision as she sobbed uncontrollably. The world and all its problems disappeared.

Her body sank into the ocean of fur and they clawed at her for attention. Thousands of nails raked across her legs, but she didn't feel it. She didn't care. They defecated on her and she sank deeper and deeper, her skin slipping from bones, the smile painted on her face, darkness suffocating her, dragging her deeper and deeper, puppies, puppies, everywhere. She wanted to tell Macy she loved her. She wanted to say she was sorry, and she wanted to stop...

CHAPTER

"I chops 'em up good, yes I do. Chop chop chop, chops 'em up good. I keep choppin', yes I do. Don't look at me while I make love to you. Chop chop chop, chop em' up good. I chops 'em up good, yes I do."

The axe fell.

LIMITED EDITION EXCLUSIVE

Brain wasn't sure if the vomit was his. When he groggily awoke next to the pile of food chunks, he wiped his mouth and found it dry. He wasn't sure where he was, and the headache was enough to make him want to go back to sleep.

When he realized he was lying in absolute darkness, he thought about Kirk's van and clutched at the soft, purple rug beneath him. Sure enough, that's where he was. He began to recall a trip to Hooksville to see the town for Jack's drug venture, but Brain had mostly wanted to see the legendary comic store where people had been skinned alive. He allowed himself to get drunk, and he regretted it. He wasn't really into alcohol because it dulled his brain, and he always wanted to be sharp. His mind was the only thing he had that was worthwhile, besides his collection of Manga books at home on his bookshelves.

He opened the van doors and stepped out. Night had fallen, leaving the deserted town clad in black. He couldn't see anything, and his foggy head obscured his vision with spots; he dizzily leaned against the rear fender and closed his eyes. He needed to sit down and figure this all out.

"Who do you want to be?"

The voice startled him, and he turned to see a shape standing two feet away from him. His eyes failed to adjust, and he shook his head. "Who…?"

76

Gentle hands landed on his shoulders and eased him back onto the fender. It was a woman, though he couldn't tell who it was.

"Think about the question and tell me," she said.

He didn't recognize the raspy voice, so he reasoned it was Miko, who up until now completely ignored him. Why did she want to talk to him? Wasn't she in the back of the van when he passed out?

"Where is everyone?" was all he could mumble.

"Where do you think?" she asked, though it barely sounded like a question.

"I don't know." He shook his head and rubbed his eyes again. "I feel like shit. I thought I saw Jack a while ago... how long was I out?"

He was sitting with Jack on the back of the van in the sunlight, and tried to remember something he said, something about Jamie and Kirk, but he lost it. Was it a dream?

"It doesn't matter," Miko said. "I want you to think about my question. I need an answer from you."

"Your question?" I don't know... I can't even think straight, I'm sorry." He suddenly realized that a beautiful girl was talking to him, and it was only easy to speak to her because she was invisible in the absolute darkness of an abandoned town.

"Maybe you're not comfortable," she said. "I'll go first. I'll let you ask me anything you want. You get what you need, but promise you'll answer my question."

He was suddenly very conscious about the smell of his breath. He put his hands on his knees and let

77

his eyes try to find her in the dark, but the headache was nearly too much for him. If he concentrated hard enough, he might be able to make a good impression on her. Why was that so important? He couldn't even hope to take her away from Jack if she was there to keep him company.

"I don't know what to say," Brain managed. "I don't even know who you are, or why you came with us. I mean, I can guess. You're with Jack, right?" he thought the question carried the weight of doom.

"No," she said.

"Uh, okay. So, like, uh, what do you do for a living? I don't mean to get personal. Okay, maybe you don't have to answer that. We're just getting to know each other and I was just thinking…"

"Shut up," she said. "I'm a dancer. You already guessed. You wanted me to say it. Ask me something you don't know. Something that might be important to you."

He sighed. "I can hardly even think straight. I got screwed up, you know. I don't know what's going on. I… shit. Okay."

"Ask me a question I might be offended by," she said, "although it's something that really wouldn't offend me or anyone else, even though you think it might. Maybe it's a question we all want someone to ask."

She was playing a game with him and it was a struggle. He wished he had Jack's charisma or Kirk's devil-may-care attitude. They would know how to talk to a girl like Miko. He felt terribly lost and confused. It was a good thing he couldn't see her. He wouldn't be able to look her in the face, and he would find himself stealing glances at her long, cinnamon legs.

"Why did you become a stripper?—I mean dancer. Sorry. Dancer. You didn't say stripper."

"That's what I am. I take my clothes off in front of people for money. I shake my ass and dance on crotches. I rub my tits all over the faces of boys just like you. Loners. Nerds. Freaks of nature. You're a smart one, aren't you? Jack calls you Brain. But you're name's Brian. Brian Powers."

"Um."

"I do it because I can. I don't have what you have. No skills. Just a body. Hated school, love to party. I partied so much it became boring. This became a way of life. A job. It's what I do. I put on makeup and lingerie like you put on a shirt and tie."

"I didn't think, uh, I mean, I didn't think you were any different. I respect you and everything. You do what you have to do for a living. You're opening up to me and everything, I mean, that's pretty cool. Uh, so do you like, uh, have kids?"

"No."

"Oh. I see. Well, I... I wanted to draw comics. When I was in school I used to draw characters all day, except when I was in math class. I'm good with numbers, you see. Really good. Well, that's why Jack calls me Brain. Anyway, I just like to read, you know? Don't draw too much anymore."

"Because you're tortured. All artists are tortured. They see things nobody else can see. You're afraid to look because nobody wants to see what you

79

see. Nobody but you. That doesn't change what you do or who you are. It's still inside of you."

Her interest in him was strange, but it felt nice for someone to ask him about the things he liked. Where was Jack? He felt like he was an uninvited guest in someone's house. He probably shouldn't even be talking to her, much less having such deep conversation. What did she want from him?

"Where did you say everyone was?" Brain asked, his head still swimming from his run-in with Captain Morgan and Mary Jane..

"At the comic store," she replied without affect, as if wasn't supposed to be a surprise.

"Without me?" Brain sat up too quickly from the fender and nearly fell flat on his face. She steadied him, and he sat back down.

"Do you want to draw another comic?" she asked. "You have characters in mind? A story?"

("You see, Doc, it all becomes academic at that point. I'm not one for romance. I don't know… I leave that to my characters. Let them fall in love."

"So what you're telling me is that she took an interest in you. I'm flipping through the pages here… can you tell me which one she is?"

"Here, let me see. Uh… right here."

"Nothing what you described earlier. She has blond hair and… she's rather…"

"It's *my* fantasy, Doc. What difference does it make, really? Not even really, because that word doesn't apply. If your dreams come true then you need another dream, another fantasy. Something else follows you through the pages of your own book and maybe you stop writing it or maybe you keep going with it and change things in a way nobody else wanted. Like a sequel that's written in first-person or a 'fresh' take on an old idea. You know how everyone complains they want something new and original but they really don't? They just want a boy and a girl to fall in love. It doesn't matter if they're aliens or vampires or if they disappear across time and space, or if they meet in each other in dreams or in the pages of a book."

"Interesting. So you made love to her?"

"I want to tell you about sunrise.")

Dawn. Cutting jaggedly through the endless morning or evening or twilight, something simple and expected. Nature's breakfast, the chirping of insects while other things die.

Brain's arm draped over the woman's chest. They lay across a pew in the broken church, with the hole in the roof exposing the dreamers to morning's light. Nothing stirred save for the fluttering of Brain's eyelids while he dreamt.

In his dream he was an artist who lay on a psychiatrist's couch with his eyes staring at the ceiling. He was a best-selling artist and storyteller, but in a fit of insanity brought on by the characters in his head who argued and battled with each other for control of the world, he chopped up Jack, Jamie, and Kirk in the back of a van while they were visiting an abandoned town called Hooksville. Brain was hypnotized by the psychiatrist in order to recall the events that led to his downward spiral. Instead, Brain recalled a dream he had. In this dream, he was in a world drawn by a Manga artist's imagination; a garden of long bamboo stalks and some of them were shorter. Impaled upon the stalks were the heads of his dead friends. They had eyes bigger than their cheeks while their hair was one solid color and spiked by an artist's propensity to wreck the theory of gravity. Brain walked through the bamboo forest while the mouths of his friends opened and said cruel things to him, though he refused to hear. When he came to the end of the forest there was a tall woman wearing thigh-high boots and a blue skirt that flared up around her waist by a wind that was relative to her alone, showing bright white panties perched between a pair of long legs. Her chest was impossibly large and her blond hair swirled around her shoulders.

When Brain awoke from his vivid experience, he sat up and looked up at the blue sky for a long time. He listened to the wind fight with the dust, and he wondered what the hell he had been doing for the last few hours.

"Your dreams are interesting," Miko said while lying on her back.

Brain shook his head. "I don't remember last night. All I remember is…" he didn't want to say. He remembered shadows and the moon, he remembered being wet, hands on his chest. An impossible ecstasy. A scream somewhere in the wilderness, either in his mind or from his lips or from elsewhere. The world fell into place around him like stardust falling from the hair of a god that had stepped out of a steamy shower.

"Why?" Brain asked. "Why would you…?" he was careful not to insult or accuse. He was treading on thin ice.

"This flesh means nothing, is nothing," Miko said. "I want your dreams and all your failings. I want what you see and how you see it. I want your fear, and I want to know how you see others' fears. Your whole life, you've been afraid to talk to women. You've isolated yourself, and now, you know it was pointless. The flesh is willing. The flesh means nothing."

She wasn't making any sense. Was she smoking more of the reefer? Jack and the others must've returned to the van by now. His headache was gone but his head felt as if a block had been placed in front of his thoughts, as if neurons terminated at the point of departure behind his eyes. He couldn't properly remember anything because he'd been too screwed up from all the marijuana and alcohol. Jack would have laughed and slapped him on the shoulder. He would have called him a 'lightweight,' even though Jack never really asked Brain to do or sell any of his drugs.

He thought his first time would've been more memorable. He heard stories about the first time being quite forgettable, and he couldn't even remember one second of it. His brain was scrambled and nothing made sense. He desperately wanted a shower.

"Okay, party's over," he said and regretted it because he sounded like a bastard. "If Jack's all done looking around, I want to get the hell out of this hole.

I've seen enough."

"He's *been* done looking around," Miko said. "You were too busy screwing around to realize it."

"Look, I'm sorry. I didn't mean anything. I just… want to leave."

"Don't you see what I mean? You're ready to move on. Are you ashamed of me? I thought maybe I would inspire you to draw again. We didn't do anything that was wrong. Humans do this. They fuck. They breed. I want you to draw."

He sighed. He wasn't sure how he felt about sex, especially because he couldn't remember it. He wasn't ashamed, nor did he feel like he wanted to try again. He knew nothing about this woman, and he was so used to his way of life. Getting up every morning to go to work, coming home from the dealership to watch cartoons, read, or play *World of Warcraft*. He couldn't imagine having a girlfriend because that would completely change his habits, and he hated change.

"Let's go back to the van," he finally said, attempting to brush aside everything she said. "Jack's probably going to have a fit because he's antsy as hell. I'm sure Kirk's been yelling at Jamie enough to make her cry a few times by now. Everything will be back to normal." He wasn't sure why he added the last part.

"They're not at the van," Miko said. "I already told you where they are."

Brain pursued his lips. He wanted to shout at her, but kept his frustration in check. "Okay. I don't remember. Where?"

"*Gravity Comics*. They've been there all night."

"What? How do you know? They wouldn't be there the whole night. All the supplies are in the van, and they never came back, unless they came back while we were here. I don't even know how I got here."

"They never came back. They're dead."

"What's the first thing that comes to mind when I ask you to picture your mother?"

"You haven't been listening, Doc. Your questions are pissing me off."

"We're trying to get right down to it. We've been going around in circles."

"You want to see if I'm sane. You're testing me. I know how all this works, Doc. If I'm capable of standing trial, then I can't plead insanity."

"People were murdered. How do you feel about that?"

"That's an ambiguous question. Rather stupid. People are murdered every day, and I don't feel a damn thing. Nobody feels anything anymore. That's the point. That's what I'm trying to tell you. They've taken art away from us, and we're looking for it in the blood where it sleeps."

"Continue."

LIKE LOLIPOPS DRESSED IN GASOLINE

Brain stood in the street and looked up at the comic store. Untouched by vandalism or fire, *Gravity Comics* was covered in dust but no worse for wear. Grime covered the windows, making it impossible to look inside. Otherwise, it squatted in the middle of the town, a forgotten landmark where a madman had committed murders.

"This town's only feature was this store," Brain commented. "People came from all over to check this place out. The guy knew everything there was to know about comics. He was an expert. I found an interview in an online newspaper, and he kept saying he actually wasn't a big fan of comics because his knowledge came from somewhere outside of him. It's the only interview anyone ever did. He was apparently a pretty mean guy." Brain sighed because he knew he was rambling.

"Are you afraid?" Miko asked. "You think he's still alive?"

Brain shrugged. "I don't see why he'd still be here if he was. When you think about it, you have to wonder why someone would even have a comic store out here in the first place. It's a pretty stupid idea from a business standpoint, but it worked out. Somehow."

There was nothing to be afraid of. His friends were inside screwing around, and Miko was still blasted out of her mind. She was a philosophical stripper, her brain likely damaged from drugs and dark rooms with

87

faceless men.

He pushed open the front door and found a man sitting in the middle of a stuffy, empty room. Sunlight from outside exploded through the gloom. Brain stopped on the threshold to breathe in the thick dust while he stood and looked at the emptiness of a myth.

"Close the damn door, will ya?"

The man in the center of the room had a voice that rumbled, and his body was larger than his words. He rose from his chair and planted his fists against his hips, rolls of fat bulging over a pair of white underwear that was barely visible beneath the wall of pale, hairy flesh. His stubby legs were pistons of hair and meat. His big face had eyes that reminded Brain of a fruit fly.

The door closed behind them, and when Miko grabbed his hand and intertwined her fingers with his, he realized how cold he felt.

"You're strong," she whispered in his ear. "You can do this."

Do what? He still wasn't sure what was happening. The big man's odor overwhelmed the dust with the smell of moldy salami soaked in garlic butter. Shards of sunlight eked through the grimy, cobwebbed windows.

"I'm just looking for my friends," Brain said. "I thought they might be here. I don't mean to intrude."

"WRONG!" the man's shout was a foghorn over labyrinthine water. "You came here for ME! Why else would you be here? I wanted to redecorate for you, but I just didn't have time. You'll have to forgive me, but I did manage to finish making my cape. Do you like it?"

While he turned around, Miko pressed something into his pocket. "You'll know what to do," she said. "I believe in you. You'll always be an artist."

On the man's back was a patchy, almost translucent cape colored in stitched patches of brown, red, and pink.

"I'm sorry," Brain said, ignoring whatever Miko put into his pocket. He started to feel nervous; he didn't belong here, and it was possible something bad happened to his friends. "We'll leave. I'm just wondering if maybe you saw my friends. If they caused any… um, well if they were a bit rowdy, I'm sorry for that."

The man was silent for a moment as he turned to face them again, and he stared for a long time. Brain felt uneasy; he could hear the man's ragged breathing as if maybe he suffered from bronchitis or some other lung problem.

"You came here for me," the man finally said. "There's no other reason why you would be here. They told me you would come and I should welcome you. They said you were an artist and I should work with you, get to know you, become your friend. I love MY friends, but you see, they're not always right. They can't be. They just can't."

"I don't know… uh, we'll just be on our way. Thanks for your time."

"Your friends are dead you fucking moron," the man wheezed. "You know who I am. Stop being stupid. You're here because you think you can run MY STORE!

89

This is what my mother GAVE TO ME!"

"Dead…"

"Dead! Dead. Dead. Dead. D-E-A-D DEAD! Chopped up, and I'm almost done working on them. They were quite a delight, you know. I suppose nobody's gonna miss 'em."

This wasn't happening. This man couldn't be real. Maybe Brain was still dreaming. He might still be lying in the back of the van, too jacked from all the booze and weed. The more he thought about it, the more that seemed likely. A pretty girl like Miko wasn't going to have sex with him or start any kind of philosophical questioning. And his friends weren't dead. Jack could never die.

The big man moved behind the old counter where fanboys would have made their purchases. Brain started to process everything; he should get the hell out, but there was something keeping him there. Miko's hand was warm, and when she looked up at him with her brown eyes and her tousled black hair, she spoke to him in a tone of voice no woman had ever shared with him.

"You're the artist now. Draw what you see and wherever you can. It's your only way out. I'll do anything to inspire you."

The big, semi-nude man suddenly stepped in front of them and roughly shoved Brain aside. The man was strong; Brain landed a few feet away on his shoulder. He thought he heard something snap, and the pain in his arm confirmed it was likely broken. He tasted dust and blood as he lay on his side in agony, clutching his shoulder while attempting to roll to his back. He lost his glasses in the dust.

He'd never broken a bone before in his life. Where was Jack to protect him?

Brain couldn't hear himself screaming over the big man's thunderous laughter.

"What a piece of shit," the man announced. "They want YOU? For what? You don't have the talent or the vision. You don't have the balls, little shit-boy. They're just testing me. This is all a test, and I'm going to just get right to work on little missy here. What with her long legs and all."

"Don't hurt her!" Brain shouted. "Please! Miko, get away! Get away!"

He was concerned for her, and he was surprised that she just stood there. The man hefted a big axe over his shoulder, and Miko didn't so much as flinch.

"The flesh is weak," she said. "Let me inspire you."

"Okay!" the man lifted his axe into the air, and Brain closed his eyes. He heard the *ka-chunk* of the axe hitting solid flesh and bone and something falling onto the floor.

"No…" Brain begged, but he knew it was no good. He really was a weakling. All his life, he'd been dependent on Jack to help him. He never put his mind to reason into or out of situations. Miko was the only girl, besides his mother, who spoke to him like he mattered. Now, she was going to die.

He tried to turn over onto his side to push himself up, but it was no good. He heard the axe fall again—*ka-chunk, ka-chunk.* It fell rhythmically, each

91

strike seconds apart. Not once did Miko scream or call out. She didn't make a sound.

Brain sobbed as he pictured Miko's face. She'd looked at him with absolute faith, a belief in who he was. She was fixated on his abilities as an artist rather than his skill with numbers, which was the only talent he had that gave him a chance to earn a living. Her odd endorsement conflicted with his sense of comfort and normalcy, but only now did he think maybe she was right. She died for him and he didn't know why. He couldn't die here with her.

"Wheeew," the man stopped hacking away. "A lot of work, boy I'll tell you what. Wonder what she would have been like, but hey, that's life. You can't be squeamish, shit-boy! In fact, I'm feeling a little bit of an *urge*, if you know what I mean. It's been a while. All work and no play... as the saying goes. Look at them legs. Yeah. I can dig this."

Brain refused to look. He couldn't stand the sight of blood, and his stomach churned as he thought about what was happening. A woman was murdered right in front of him, chopped into pieces by a maniac. Crying was no use. He had to do *something*. He felt around in his pocket for whatever Miko put there; it had to be important.

It was a simple black pen.

Let me inspire you. Draw what you see.

He scooted sideways so he could see what was happening. He prepared himself for a gory scene, though he told himself he would do whatever he could to avoid looking at Miko.

The big man held Miko's head by the hair, blood dripping from the stump of the neck. Sour bile rose and forced its way through Brain's throat, though he swallowed it down fast enough so he wouldn't choke. He opened his eyes again and saw the killer slip his underwear down to his ankles and place the head against his crotch.

"That's the way," the big man said. "Yesssss... that's it, baby. You know what I like."

Draw what you see.

Brain began to scribble the likeness of the killer on the inside of his arm. What else was he going to do? Miko's last words seemed significant somehow, as if she were reaching out to him through the realm of death before she'd been killed. He did his best not to look directly at the killer, but he conjured the image from everything he saw. While the killer groaned and shuddered, Brain drew as fast as he could. But he needed his glasses. He needed to draw everything he saw. That's what Miko told him to do.

He patted around the floor with his hand, stretching out while something crawled over his fingertips. There. His glasses.

"Almost there..." the axe-murderer grunted.

Yes, he was a good artist. Even on his arm, the portrait took shape in the darkness. He angled his flesh into the orange glow that penetrated the yellow, flaking dirt on the windows. Every inch counted; Brain pushed against the floorboards with his feet, his shoulder burning with fresh pain. He gritted his teeth so he wouldn't attract attention; he stifled each yelp of pain as

93

he turned his arm and scribbled. He pressed the pen into his skin, tattooing himself with a picture of the big man's head, drawing blood from fresh wounds. Brain breathed through his teeth, his chest rising and falling, his concentration nearly failing. The pain was too much, but he couldn't pass out. He was a man possessed; this was something that felt right, a pain he needed. He would torture himself for the sake of art before the axe fell upon his neck, and it felt *right*.

"Baby! Yes! That's it! More, do it, more, do it, YEAH! OH YEAH!"

A loud crash diverted Brain's attention. He looked up and saw the killer stagger backward against the counter, dropping Miko's bloody head; luckily, a thick patch of darkness between the big man's legs obscured whatever might be hanging there.

"What...?" the man shook his head as if he'd been slapped hard in the face.

A powerful sound pulsed through Brain's head, and he nearly dropped the pen. He breathed deeply, inhaling as he tried to keep his focus on the task. The noise throbbed like a voice mumbling against a pillow.

Molb, molb, molb, molb, molb, molb...

"No!" the killer tried to steady himself against the counter. "Stay away! I'm not FINISHED! You can't tell me... it's not true!" He pressed his palms against his temples and fell again, his weight causing him to lose the battle for balance with his underwear cuffing his ankles.

Molb, molb, molb, molb, molb, molb...

"Superman is not better than Batman!" the

94

killer shouted, slamming his fists on the floorboards like a petulant child. "Batman's an avenger of the night, a skilled detective. He beats Superman in a fight! He's smarter and faster.''

The severed limbs leapt up as if pulled by a puppet master's strings. They danced through the dust, the feet moving in tune to the terrible sound. Fingers clutched at air while the torso joined in. Miko's head bounced along to the beat, too, as a thick liquid dribbled out of her open mouth.

"Batman isn't realistic," Brain declared. "Superman has other-worldly powers. Batman's a millionaire ninja with a bunch of gadgets. Anyone can be Batman. Not everyone can be Superman. Supes is the American dream. He fights for truth and justice unselfishly—"

"NOOOOOOO!!!!" The big man squealed. "You lie! LIE!"

Molb, molb, molb, molb, molb, molb…

Brain poked at his flesh with the pen, doing his best to add details to the face. Miko's bits kept dancing around, and Brain just needed to keep working. He was almost finished. A little bit more light.

"This is MY store!" the big man rose to his feet, lifting the axe along with his bulging belly. "I'm not tired. I'm not! You puny little shit-boy. Do you know who I AM? DO YOU?"

The killer turned around to the counter and braced himself. Dropping the axe, he decisively grabbed a marker and started to scribble all over the counter. "I'm faster than you! I'm better than you! I've created a masterpiece with my blood and sweat, and you'll never take it from me!"

Now the sound was louder, and Brain did all he could to look away from the eerily dancing limbs. Blood from his arm soaked into the dust and his vision blurred. He was losing blood, and he did all he could to make sure he wasn't cutting through a vein.

MOLB, MOLB, MOLB, MOLB, MOLB, MOLB...

The door exploded off its hinges, bathing the entire store in eye-searing light. The big man roared and brought his thick forearm up in front of his face. Finally, Brain could see everything. Hot wind picked up dust and swirled it around, and he had to close his eyes and mouth to keep from being suffocated. The windows shattered, the grime-stained glass raining shards. Brain saw Miko behind his eyes, looking up at him, imploring him to go on, to sacrifice his soul for the sake of art.

He wasn't sure if he opened his eyes at all. Blue light soaked through his vision and the throbbing noise filled his head. "Superman," he cried out. "The light…"

"AAAAAAAAAAAAAAAAAAAAAAAAAAAAAAAAAA AHHHHHHHHHHHHHH!" the murderer screamed.

(*Shapes dancing through the shadows. Figures clad in latex. Capes billowing.*

"I need your brain this time," Jack said. "We're going to make this thing happen. Roll in the millions. Hooksville is going to be perfect."

MOLB,MOLB, MOLB.

"Batman should be shot in the head. He can't

96

dodge bullets. He's just a man. Superman is more than a man. He's every man."

"The flesh is weak."

Their hands are upon him. Trapped somewhere between the image and the nightmare, reality spinning on threads, Miko's pieces jumping for joy. How do we know it's joy? We know everything. We'll take care of Damien. Take him away forever. His time has passed. We seek the power of the sane.

Entertainment. Fear is art, fear is blood and beauty and art so beautiful, so wonderful it's tragic but here we are between phases of the moon or sun.

"I don't need you anymore, Brain. You're out of this deal. Thanks for showing me the place. You can't get wrapped up in it. Your little world of numbers and masturbating. Give yourself a round of applause."

YES. YES. A round of applause for the artist.

"I'm not really here now. Someone else knows my name."

"YOU CAN'T TAKE ME! No. No. NOOOOOOOOOOOOOOOOO!"

The heart bleeds. Listen for it.

MOLB, MOLB, MOLB.

The cape demonstrates his majesty. He is the every man. The power of the sun compels him. The power of light and truth. He doesn't hide from the dark but dispels it, conquers it with his vision of justice and morality.

"FUCKING… NO! NOT HIM! ANYBODY BUT HIM!"

"Draw what you see."

"ROBIN, HELP ME! Mother, I did what you told me. I did what everyone told me. It doesn't hurt you piece of SHIT. Is that all you got? IS THAT ALL YOU GOT?")

TO UNDERSTAND THE GRAVITY OF
THE SITUATION

She crossed one long leg over the other, swinging her foot while she tapped her pen against her notepad, the comic book on her lap sprawled open to the last page.

"Your comic is rather interesting," she said.

"I think Brain will do, Doc," he said and sat up on the couch. "If you let me draw a picture of you, I think you'll understand how everything works."

"How do you feel when you look at me?" she asked.

Pencil-thin skirt hugging her thighs, black stockings and heels. Glasses perched upon her nose, a hint of the exotic in her long lashes and dark flesh. She was a bit young to be a doctor, but he often thought about her when he sat up at night and pored over the pages of his latest work. She inspired him, but all he could draw was a busty blonde in a cheerleader outfit.

He shook his head. "I don't want my job back. I like what I do. I like being an artist."

Mother had been angry with him. They fought over his career decision over and over again, even though all she ever wanted was for him to be happy. He'd never argued with her before, and it felt good. He wanted to tell his doctor which character in his comic was supposed to be his mother, but he thought better of it.

99

"How do you feel when you look at me?" she asked again.

"Well, you know, I want to… I mean, it's been a while for me, but… Jack, see, Jack… he wanted me to be happy. I think that's what he wanted. I could never tell. He seemed to always have good intentions. I miss him. Whatever they found in my apartment, I mean, I know it was a mess, because you see, I'm still kind of sloppy with the axe."

"How do you feel when you look at me?"

She stood then and dropped the notepad onto her chair. He looked at the name on the desk and scratched at his scarred left arm.

Miko removed her glasses and dropped them onto the notepad. "The flesh is weak," she said. "I know you want to hurt me. To chop me into little pieces. What will you do with me after? Are you going to be a messy boy?"

Brain swallowed. A beautiful girl like her never should have been talking to him, unless she was a doctor. Unless he was ordered by the court to talk so they could find out if he was insane. But they didn't handcuff him. The legal system didn't bring him here. Who did?

Miko brought her fingertips to the top of her forehead and traced them vertically down the length of her body. *Zip.* The skin flopped away like a cheap Halloween costume. Another woman stepped out of the body suit, a woman that looked nothing like Miko at all.

Frazzled gray hair, thin lips drawn tightly over a square chin. Her body frail and thin with bright white

100

flesh. She wore a blue gown, and she reached back to the couch and picked up the pen.

He couldn't believe it. After all this time. She was supposed to be locked away in a mental institution, drooling and rambling while aliens circled around her head and promised nightmares.

"I want you to have this pen," Robin Shears said.

Brian Powers heard a noise that warmed his skull and caused the skin on his arms to tingle.

"You've seen my art," the mother of a notorious axe-murderer said, her voice shaking from years of disuse. "Show me if you can bleed the way I do."

Then, her mouth moved, and all around him, the noise was loud and clear.

Molb, molb, molb, molb,molb, molb…

deleted scene

"Special edition comics are a gimmick."

Brian looked up at Mom, wondering if the conversation between the two men was going to influence her; she might keep him from buying the Superman comic that was behind the counter. She'd promised he could have it if he saved his money from doing chores around the house. For almost a year, he saved up, dreaming of the moment he would approach the counter, beaming with a smile on his face. He couldn't wait to tell the man behind the counter he was finally going to buy it. Finally.

The Death of Superman with the limited edition holofoil cover.

Hopefully, nobody bought it. After a year of saving, he couldn't imagine how he would feel if somebody else bought it, first.

But two guys were talking loudly, their voices carrying over the boxes that were packed with comics tucked snugly in their plastic shields, the white backboards preventing them from being bent.

"Yeah, I don't buy special editions. A ripoff. Defeats the purpose of reading comics. I buy them for the stories, you know?"

The other man nodded.

"I don't think this is a good idea," Mom said.

No. It was happening. Brian had to have the comic.

Gravity Comics was the best comic store in the

state, even if the man behind the counter was an asshole. Nobody else had the Superman comic Brian wanted. Buying the rare book was an adventure; scrubbing dishes, cleaning up dog shit, taking out the trash. All he had to do was keep Mom convinced it was a good idea.

And the mean guy was behind the counter. Doodling on his sketchpad like he always did. The owner of Gravity Comics.

Mom hated him.

He had to be brave. The man was going to make fun of him, maybe try to convince him that Superman was a shitty character. For too long, he'd been dreaming about this moment. The man never thought he was going to buy the comic. Not in a million years.

Mr. Shears looked up at him, a smile touching the corners of his face. His eyebrows darted up to in pyramid configurations. Mom said he looked like a fat Jack Nicholson.

"Look who it is," Mr. Shears dropped his pen onto the sketchpad.

"Hello," Mom tried to be friendly.

"I'm glad you're here today," Mr. Shears licked his lips and mocked them with false courtesy. "You should know we're going to stop selling Superman comics. No more Superman. I've also contacted DC and told them to stop making them. Or at least, they should do another fight with Batman, because Batman always wins. If they don't make the comic…" he drew his thumb across his neck in a mock-slash.

"Did somebody already buy it?" Mom's voice shook like a penny in a jar.

"Nobody buys Superman. Superman sucks. Everyone knows that."

Brian had argued with some of his classmates about the same topic over and over again, and he could always convince them that Batman was inferior. If only he was brave enough to stand up to Mr. Shears...

"I don't know why we keep coming back here," Mom said.

"To please your pussy of a son," Mr. Shears said. "You think I need your business? I've got the biggest comic store in Arizona. Nobody sells more Batman or X-Men than I do."

Now was the time to strike. One day, he could write and draw his own comic about this moment, the day he bought The Death of Superman from Mr. Shears.

"I've got the money."

Mr. Shears stared at him. He straightened to his full height, his broad shoulders blocking the display of expensive, rare comics behind him.

Brian swallowed. Mom adjusted the glasses on the bridge of her nose; she wasn't going to be any help. She didn't like Mr. Shears, and wasn't about to stand up to him. She knew how much Brian loved coming to this store. She would never spoil this moment.

"I'm not selling it."

The other customers in the store weren't talking anymore, and Brian was afraid they could hear his heart beating. How many times had Mr. Shears been nasty to them, too? They should be on his side, standing up for him.

"I've got the money," Brian said.

"I heard you the first time, you little twit," Mr. Shears stepped back from the display behind him.

There it was. The Death of Superman, limited edition holofoil cover.

But there was something different about it this time.

It was autographed.

"In your wildest dreams," Mr. Shears said.

***

"Brian, will you allow me to comment on the content of this piece?"

"I don't think you're qualified to judge art, but go ahead."

"Not qualified?"

"You wanted to know about my mother, so then I start talking about her and you interrupted me. That's rude."

"That has nothing to do with my qualifications."

"I don't want to talk about my mother anymore."

"We were making progress…"

"Were we?"

"I just want to figure out how this scene fits into the story. I was under the impression that you've been to Gravity Comics before, but at the end of the story, you meet Damien Shears and you act like you've never seen him before. He acts like he has no idea who you are. So are you adding a scene to your story, and throwing your mother in just to appease me?"

"Do you think she's pretty?"

105

"She looks like Miko. An older Miko."

"What do you mean? Miko's Asian. My mom wasn't Asian."

"The style. I'm talking about the style."

"Now you're a critic. Did we already talk about your qualifications?"

"Well. This is issue number zero, right? A special edition?"

"Zero issues aren't special editions. You don't know anything about comics."

***

Brian withdrew the wad of cash from his pocket.

"Do you have any idea how many people I've killed here?" Mr. Shears asked.

The sketchpad was lying open on the counter, and Brian could see what Mr. Shears had been working on. He felt like a part of his head was opening up and an idea was being placed inside like a corner puzzle piece that had fallen onto the floor from the table, a piece that had been sought after for hours, the perpetrator of frustration and arguments about whether or not the entire puzzle should be disassembled and returned to the store, or, at the very least, the phone number on the box should be called and the piece should be sent to them for free (but, there wasn't a number on the box to call).

Brian wasn't thinking about puzzles or puzzle pieces, because Mr. Shears was standing back from the counter as if inviting Brian to look upon the art.

"I don't kill people because I want to," Mr.

106

Shears said. "I kill them because I'm supposed to."

For a moment, Brian forgot about the Superman comic, and he forgot anyone else was in the store. On the sketchpad was the rough draft of a comic that featured people browsing for comic books in a comic book store. There was enough detail for Brian to recognize the characters. In one of the panels were the two men who'd been talking about limited edition books. Another panel showed Brian standing alone with money at his feet.

"You're pretty good," Brian said.

"I know I'm good. I'm the best, and that's why I've been asked to kill people."

"I draw too, but I like to do something more like Anime."

"That shit's too easy. You're telling me you draw Superman comics with an Anime style?"

Mr. Shears chuckled. Both hands were on his shaking belly. Brian could see the sweat stains in the armpits of his shirt.

The money wasn't in Brian's hand anymore. Did he put it back in his pocket? He tried to peer over Mr. Shears' shoulders for another glimpse of the Superman book. The rare holofoil cover. He'd worked so hard to buy it. He wasn't afraid of Mr. Shears; he was just another artist who couldn't make it and treated people like dirt. He was just another dreamer.

"Why do you like Batman so much?" Brian asked. Maybe if he sucked up enough, Mr. Shears would stop acting like a jackass. Every artist had an ego.

Mr. Shears stopped laughing and his eyebrows

scrunched together. "You have no idea what you're asking, you little shit. LOOK AROUND YOU! THIS IS REAL ART!"

All the tables and their boxes full of comics were gone. Bare floorboards replaced carpet. The windows were covered in pale, leathery drapes that looked like snakeskin.

Sunlight against the strange curtains shifted the spectrum of colors between gold and red, brown and white. The store smelled like wet cardboard.

Brian's worst fear was coming true. Too many times, he had nightmares about his mom pulling into a parking space in the street. They would be sitting in the car and looking at the CLOSED sign in the front window.

"No," Brian said.

"What did you expect me to do? You would do the same thing if you were me. Listen, you little brat— I'm an artist. I decorate in my spare time. My mother usually expects me to bring my work home with me, but I'm FREE to to do the art I've always wanted to do! Mother wishes she was half the artist I am. So I had her locked up in the loony bin…"

There wasn't a single comic in the store. Nothing behind the counter.

"Not even the aliens can tell me what to do! And this is what happens to fools who don't understand comics! These idiots didn't understand ART!"

Mr. Shears pointed to his sketchpad at the two men who had been badmouthing special editions.

Brian's hands searched his pockets for the
108

money again. Maybe Mom had it in the car with her.

"You wish you could draw like me," Mr. Shears said. "This is natural talent, like I said. If mother were here, she would suggest I include you, BUT SHE'S A LUNATIC! If she had half a brain, she would have told the aliens to kill all the dumb brats who prefer to draw Anime garbage."

Brian looked at the drapes and wondered if his mom worried about him.

"Um, I want to buy The Death of Superman limited edition with the holofoil cover."

***

"You were there when he killed those people? He let you live? That would explain why you wanted to go back with your friends."

"You have no idea what you're talking about."

"Damien Shears was talking about his mother. You deflected my question, and you changed the story."

"Shit."

About the Author

Vincenzo Bilof is a professional scuba diver; he is the recipient of the COMEBACK SCUBA DIVER OF THE YEAR award in 1996. He sometimes sleeps in Michigan.

Gravity Comics Massacre

www.ingramcontent.com/pod-product-compliance
Lightning Source LLC
Chambersburg PA
CBHW070630130626
46555CB00006B/2503